TIME AND CHANGE
BY
JOHN BUR

PREFACE

I suspect that in this volume my reader will feel that I have given him a stone when he asked for bread, and his feeling in this respect will need no apology. I fear there is more of the matter of hard science and of scientific speculation in this collection than of spiritual and aesthetic nutriment; but I do hope the volume is not entirely destitute of the latter. If I have not in some degree succeeded in transmuting my rocks into a kind of wholesome literary bread, or, to vary the figure, in turning them into a soil in which some green thing or flower of human interest and emotion may take root and grow, then, indeed, have I come short of the end I had in view.

I am well aware that my own interest in geology far outruns my knowledge, but if I can in some degree kindle that interest in my reader, I shall be putting him on the road to a fuller knowledge than I possess. As with other phases of nature, I have probably loved the rocks more than I have studied them. In my youth I delighted in lingering about and beneath the ledges of my native hills, partly in the spirit of adventure and a boy's love of the wild, and partly with an eye to their curious forms, and the evidences of immense time that looked out from their gray and crumbling fronts. I was in the presence of Geologic Time, and was impressed by the scarred and lichen-coated veteran without knowing who or what he was. But he put a spell upon me that has deepened as the years have passed, and now my boyhood ledges are more interesting to me than ever.

If one gains an interest in the history of the earth, he is quite sure to gain an interest in the history of the life on the earth. If the former illustrates the theory of development, so must the latter. The geologist is pretty sure to be an evolutionist. As science turns over the leaves of the great rocky volume, it sees the imprint of animals and plants upon them and it traces their changes and the appearance of new species from age to age. The biologic tree has grown and developed as the geologic soil in which it is rooted has deepened and ripened. I am sure I was an evolutionist in the abstract, or by the quality and complexion of my mind, before I read Darwin, but to become an evolutionist in the concrete, and accept the doctrine of the animal origin of man, has not for me been an easy matter.

The essays on the subject in this volume are the outcome of the stages of brooding and thinking which I have gone through in accepting this doctrine. I am aware that there is much repetition in them, but maybe on that very account they will help my reader to go along with me over the long road we have to travel to reach this conclusion.

July, 1912.

CONTENTS

TIME AND CHANGE

I

THE LONG ROAD

I

The long road I have in mind is the long road of evolution,—the road you and I have traveled in the guise of humbler organisms, from the first unicellular life in the old Cambrian seas to the complex and highly specialized creature that rules supreme in the animal kingdom to-day. Surely a long journey, stretching through immeasurable epochs of geologic time, and attended by vicissitudes of which we can form but feeble conceptions.

The majority of readers, I fancy, are not yet ready to admit that they, or any of their forebears, have ever made such a journey. We have all long been taught that our race was started upon its career only a few thousand years ago, started, not amid the warrings of savage elemental nature, but in a pleasant garden with everything needed close at hand. This belief has faded a good deal in our time, especially among thoughtful persons; but in a modified form, as the special creation theory, it held sway in the minds of the older naturalists like Agassiz and Dawson, long after Darwin had launched his revolutionary doctrine of our animal origin, putting man in the same zoological scheme as the lower orders.

We are slow to adjust our minds to the revelations of science, they have been so long adjusted to a revelation, so-called, of an entirely different character. It gives them a wrench more or less violent when we try to make them at home and at their ease amid these new and startling disclosures. To many good people evolution seems an ungodly doctrine, like setting up a remorseless logic in the place of an omnipresent Creator, But there is no help for it. Science has fairly turned us out of our comfortable little anthropomorphic notion of things into the great out-of-doors of the universe. We must and will get used to the chill, yea, to the cosmic chill, if need be. Our religious instincts will be all the hardier for it.

When we accepted Newton's discovery of the force called gravitation, we virtually surrendered ourselves to the enemy, and started upon a road, the road of natural causation, that traverses the whole system of created things. We cannot turn back; we may lie down by the roadside and dream our old dreams, but our children and their children will press on, and will be exhilarated by the journey.

It is at first sight an unpalatable truth that evolution confronts us with, and it requires courage calmly to face it. But it is in perfect keeping with the whole career of physical science, which is forever directing our attention to common near-at-hand facts for the key to remote and mysterious occurrences.

It seems to me that evolution adds greatly to the wonder of life, because it takes it out of the realm of the arbitrary, the exceptional, and links it to the sequence of natural causation. That man should have been brought into existence by the fiat of an omnipotent power is less an occasion for wonder than that he should have worked his way up from the lower non-human forms. That the manward impulse should never have been lost in all the appalling vicissitudes of geologic time, that it should have pushed steadily on, through mollusk and fish and amphibian and reptile, through swimming and creeping and climbing things, and that the forms that conveyed it should have escaped the devouring monsters of the earth, sea, and air till it came to its full estate in a human being, is the wonder of wonders.

In like manner, evolution raises immensely the value of the biological processes that are everywhere operative about us, by showing us that these processes are the channels through which the creative energy has worked, and is still working. Not in the far-off or in the exceptional does it seek the key to man's origin, but in the sleepless activity of the creative force, which has been pushing onward and upward, from the remotest time, till it has come to full fruition in man.

It is easy to inject into man's natural history a supernatural element, as nearly all biologists and anthropologists before Darwin's time did, and as many serious people still do. It is too easy, in fact, and the temptation to do so is great. It makes short work of the problem of man's origin, and saves a deal of trouble. But this method is more and more discredited, and the younger biologists and natural philosophers accept the zoological conception of man, which links him with all the lower forms, and proceed to work from that.

When we have taken the first step in trying to solve the problem of man's origin, where can we stop? Can we find any point in his history where we can say, Here his natural history ends, and his supernatural history begins? Does his natural history end with the pre-glacial man, with the cave man, or the river-drift man, with the low-browed, long-jawed fossil man of Java,—Pithecanthropus erectus, described by Du Bois? Where shall we stop on his trail? I had almost said "step on his tail," for we undoubtedly, if we go back far enough, come to a time when man had a tail. Every unborn child at a certain stage of its development still has a tail, as it also has a coat of hair and a hand-like foot. But could we stop with the tailed man—the manlike ape, or the apelike man? Did his Creator start him with this appendage, or was it a later suffix of his own invention?

If we once seriously undertake to solve the riddle of man's origin, and go back along the line of his descent, I doubt if we can find the point, or the form, where the natural is supplanted by the supernatural as it is called, where causation ends and miracle begins. Even the first dawn of protozoic life in the primordial seas must have been natural, or it would not have occurred,—must have been potential in what went before it. In this universe, so far as we know it, one thing springs from another; the sequence of cause and effect is continuous and inviolable.

We know that no man is born of full stature, with his hat and boots on; we know that he grows from an infant, and we know the infant grows from a fetus, and that the fetus grows from a bit of nucleated protoplasm in the mother's womb. Why may not the race of man grow from a like simple beginning? It seems to be the order of nature; it IS the order of nature,—first the germ, the inception, then the slow growth from the simple to the complex. It is the order of our own thoughts, our own arts, our own civilization, our own language.

In our candid moments we acknowledge the animal in ourselves and in our neighbors,—especially in our neighbors,—the beast, the shark, the hog, the sloth, the fox, the monkey; but to accept the notion of our animal origin, that gives us pause. To believe that our remote ancestor, no matter how remote in time or space, was a lowly organized creature living in the primordial seas with no more brains than a shovel-nosed shark or a gar-pike, puts our scientific faith to severe test.

Think of it. For countless ages, millions upon millions of years, we see the earth swarming with life, low bestial life, devouring and devoured, myriads of forms, all in bondage to nature or natural forces, living only to eat and to breed, localized, dependent upon place and clime, shaped to specific ends like machines,—to fly, to swim, to climb, to run, to dig, to drill, to weave, to wade, to graze, to crush,— knowing not what they do, as void of conscious purpose as the thorns, the stings, the hooks, the coils, and the wings in the vegetable world, making no impression upon the face of nature, as much a part of it as the trees and the stones, species after species having its day, and then passing off the stage, when suddenly, in the day before yesterday in the geologic year, so suddenly as to give some color of truth to the special creation theory, a new and strange animal appears, with new and strange powers, separated from the others by what appears an impassable gulf, less specialized in his bodily powers than the others, but vastly more specialized in his brain and mental powers, instituting a new order of things upon the earth, the face of which he in time changes through his new gift of reason, inventing tools and weapons and language, harnessing the physical forces to his own ends, and putting all things under his feet,—man the wonder-worker, the beholder of the stars, the critic and spectator of creation itself, the thinker of the thoughts of God, the worshiper, the devotee, the hero, spreading rapidly over the earth, and developing with prodigious strides when once fairly launched upon his career. Can it be possible, we ask, that this god was fathered by the low bestial orders below him,—instinct giving birth to reason, animal ferocity developing into human benevolence, the slums of nature sending forth the ruler of the earth. It is a hard proposition, I say, undoubtedly the hardest that science has ever confronted us with.

Haeckel, discussing this subject, suggests that it is the parvenu in us that is reluctant to own our lowly progenitors, the pride of family and position, like that of would-be aristocratic sons who conceal the humble origin of their parents. But it is more than that; it is the old difficulty of walking by faith where there is nothing visible to walk upon: we lack faith in the efficiency of the biologic laws, or any mundane forces, to bridge the tremendous chasm that separates man from even the highest of the lower orders. His radical unlikeness to all the forms below him, as if he moved in a world apart, into which they could never enter, as in a sense he does, is where the difficulty lies. Moreover, evolution balks us because of the inconceivable stretch of time during which it has been at work. It is as impossible for us to grasp geological time as sidereal space. All the standards of measurement furnished us by experience are as inadequate as is a child's cup to measure the ocean.

Several million years, or one million years,—how can we take it in? We cannot. A hundred years is a long time in human history, and how we pause before a thousand! Then think of ten thousand, of fifty thousand, of one hundred thousand, of ten hundred thousand, or one million, or of one hundred million! What might not the slow but ceaseless creative energy do in that time, changing but a hair in each generation! If our millionaires had to earn their wealth cent by cent, and carry each cent home with them at night, it would be some years before they became millionaires. This is but a faint symbol of the slow process by which nature has piled up her riches. She has had no visions of sudden wealth. To clothe the earth with soil made from the disintegrated mountains—can we figure that time to ourselves? The Orientals try to get a hint of eternity by saying that when the Himalayas have been ground to powder by allowing a gauze veil to float against them once in a thousand years, eternity will only have just begun. Our mountains have been pulverized by a process almost as slow. In our case the gauze veil is the air, and the rains, and the snows, before which even granite crumbles. See what the god of erosion, in the shape of water, has done in the river valleys and gorges—cut a mile deep in the Colorado canyon, and yet this canyon is but of yesterday in geologic time. Only give the evolutionary god time enough and all these miracles are surely wrought.

Truly it is hard for us to realize what a part time has played in the earth's history,—just time, duration,—so slowly, oh, so slowly, have the great changes been brought about! The turning of mud and silt into rock in the bottom of the old seas seems to have been merely a question of time. Mud does not become rock in man's time, nor vegetable matter become coal. These processes are too slow for us. The flexing and folding of the rocky strata, miles deep, under an even pressure, is only a question of time. Allow time enough and force enough, and a layer of granite may be bent like a bow. The crystals of the rock seem to adjust themselves to the strain, and to take up new positions, just as they do, much more rapidly, in a cake of ice under pressure. Probably no human agency could flex a stratum of rock, because there is not time enough, even if there were power enough. "A low temperature acting gradually," says my geology, "during an indefinite age would produce results that could not be otherwise brought about even through greater heat." "Give us time," say the great mechanical forces, "and we will show you the

3

immobile rocks and your rigid mountain chains as flexible as a piece of leather." "Give us time," say the dews and the rains and the snowflakes, "and we will make you a garden out of those same stubborn rocks and frowning ledges." "Give us time," says Life, starting with her protozoans in the old Cambrian seas, "and I will not stop till I have peopled the earth with myriad forms and crowned them all with man."

Dana thinks that had "a man been living during the changes that produced the coal, he would not have suspected their progress," so slow and quiet were they. It is probable that parts of our own sea-coast are sinking and other parts rising as rapidly as the oscillation of the land and sea went on that resulted in the laying down of the coal measures.

An eternity to man is but a day in the cosmic process. In the face of geologic time, man's appearance upon the earth as man, with a written history, is something that has just happened; it was in this morning's paper, we read of it at breakfast. As evolution goes, it will not be old news yet for a hundred thousand years or so, and by that time, what will he have done, if he goes on at his present rate of accelerated speed? Probably he will not have caught the gods of evolution at their work, or witnessed the origin of species by natural descent, these things are too slow for him; but he will certainly have found out many things that we are all eager to know.

In nature as a whole we see results and not processes. We see the rock strata bent and folded, we see the whole mountain-chains flexed and shortened by the flexure; but had we been present, we should not have suspected what was going on. Our little span of life does not give us the parallax necessary. The rock strata, miles thick, may be being flexed now under our feet, and we know it not. The earth is shrinking, but so slowly! When, under the slow strain, the strata suddenly give way or sink, and an earthquake results, then we know something has happened.

A recent biologist and physicist thinks, and doubtless thinks wisely, that the reason why we have never been able to produce living from non-living matter in our laboratories, is that we cannot take time enough. Even if we could bring about the conditions of the early geologic ages in which life had its dawn, which of course we cannot, we could not produce life because we have not geologic time at our disposal.

The reaction which we call life was probably as much a cosmic or geologic event as were the reactions which produced the different elements and compounds, and demanded the same slow gestation in the womb of time. During what cycles upon cycles the great mother-forces of the universe must have brooded over the inorganic before the organic was brought forth! The archean age, during which the brooding seems to have gone on, was probably as long as all the ages since.

How we are baffled when we talk about the beginning of anything in nature or in our own lives! In our experience there must be a first, but when did manhood begin; when did puberty, when did old age, begin? When did each stage of our mental growth begin? When or where did the English language begin, or the French, or the German? Was there a first English word spoken? From the first animal sound, if we can conceive of such, up to the human speech of to-day, there is an infinite gradation of sounds and words.

Was there a first summer, a first winter, a first spring? There could hardly have been a first day even for ages and ages, but only slowly approximating day. After an immense lapse of time the air must have cleared and the day become separated from the night, and the seasons must have become gradually defined. Things slowly emerge one after another from a dim, nebulous condition, both in our own growth and experience and in the development of the physical universe.

In nature there is no first and last. There is an endless beginning and an endless ending. There was no first man or first woman, no first bird, or fish, or reptile. Back of each one stretches an endless chain of approximating men and birds and reptiles.

This talk about the time and place where man began his existence seems to me misleading, because it appears to convey the idea that he began as man at some time, in some place. Whereas he grew. He began where and when the first cell appeared, and he has been on the road ever since. There is no point in the line where he emerged from the not-man and became man. He was emerging from the not-man for millions of years, and when you put your finger on an animal form and say, This is man, you must go back through whole geologic periods before you reach the not-man. If Darwin is right, there is no more reason for believing that the different species or forms of animal life were suddenly introduced than there is for believing that the soil, or the minerals, gold, silver, diamonds, or vegetable mold and verdure were suddenly introduced.

II

If we know anything of the earth's past history, we know that the continents were long in forming, that they passed through many vicissitudes of heat and cold, of fire and flood, of upheaval and subsidence—that they had, so to speak, their first low, simple rudimentary or invertebrate life, that they were all slow in getting their backbones, slower still in clothing their rock ribs with soil and verdure, that

4

they passed through a sort of amphibian stage, now under water, now on dry land, that their many kinds of soils and climes were not differentiated and their complex water-systems established till well into Tertiary times—in short, that they have passed more and more from the simple to the complex, from the disorganized to the organized. When man comes to draw his sustenance from their breasts, may they not be said to have reached the mammalian stage?

The fertile plain and valley and the rounded hill are of slow growth, immensely slow. But any given stage of the earth has followed naturally from the previous stage, only more and more and higher and higher forces took a hand in the game. First its elements passed through the stage of fire, then through the stage of water, then merged into the stage of air. More and more the aerial elements—oxygen, carbon, nitrogen—have entered into its constituents and fattened the soil. The humanizing of the earth has been largely a process of oxidation. More than disintegrated rock makes up the soil; the air and the rains and the snows have all contributed a share.

The history of the soil which we turn with our spade, and stamp with our shoes, covers millions upon millions of years. It is the ashes of the mountains, the leavings of untold generations of animal and vegetable life. It came out of the sea, it drifted from the heavens; it flowed out from the fiery heart of the globe; it has been worked over and over by frost and flood, blown by winds, shoveled by ice, —mixed and kneaded and moulded as the house-wife kneads and moulds her bread,—refining and refining from age to age. Much of it was held in solution in the primordial seas, whence it was filtered and used and precipitated by countless forms of marine life, making a sediment that in time became rocks, that again in time became continents or parts of them, which the aerial forces reduced to soil. Indeed, the soil itself is an evolution, as much so as the life upon it.

We probably have little conception of how intimate and cooperative all parts of the universe are with one another,—of the debt we owe to the farthest stars, and to the remotest period of time. We must owe a debt to the monsters of Mesozoic and Caenozoic time; they helped to fertilize the soil for us, and to discipline the ruder forces of life. We owe a debt to all that has gone before: to the heavens above and to the earth-fires beneath, to the ice-sheets that ground down the mountains, and to the ocean currents. Just as we owe a debt to the men and women in our line of descent, so we owe a debt to the ruder primordial forces that shaped the planet to our use, and took a hand in the game of animal life.

The gods of evolution had served a long apprenticeship; they had gained proficiency and were master workmen. Or shall we say that the elements of life had become more plastic and adaptable, or that the life fund had accumulated, so to speak? Had the vast succession of living beings, the long experience in organization, at last made the problem of the origin of man easier to solve?

One fancies every living thing as not only returning its mineral elements to the soil, but as in some subtle way leaving its vital forces also, and thus contributing to the impalpable, invisible store-house of vital energy of the globe.

At first among the mammalian tribes there was much muscle and little brains. But in the middle Tertiary the mammal brain began suddenly to enlarge, so that in our time the brain of the horse is more than eight times the size of the brain of his progenitor, the dinoceras of Eocene times.

Nature seems to have experimented with brains and nerve ganglia, as she has with so many other things. The huge reptilian creatures of Mesozoic time—the various dinosaurs—had ridiculously small heads and brains, but they had what might be called supplementary brains well toward the other end of the body,—great nervous masses near the sacrum, many times the size of the ostensible brain, which no doubt performed certain brain functions. But the principle of centralization was at work, and when in later time we reach the higher mammalian forms, we find these outlying nervous masses called in, so to speak, and concentrated in the head.

Nature has tried the big, the gigantic, over and over, and then abandoned it. In Carboniferous times there was a gigantic dragon-fly, measuring more than two feet in the expanse of wings. Still earlier, there were gigantic mollusks and sea scorpions, a cephalopod larger than a man; then gigantic fishes and amphibians and reptiles, followed by enormous mammals. But the geologic record shows that these huge forms did not continue. The mollusks that last unchanged through millions of years are the clam and the oyster of our day. The huge mosses and tree-ferns are gone, and only their humbler types remain. Among men giants are short-lived.

On the other hand, the steady increase in size of certain other species of animals during the later geologic ages is a curious and interesting fact. The first progenitors of the elephant that have been found show a small animal that steadily grew through the ages till the animal as we now find it is reached. Among the invertebrates this same progressive increase in size has been noted, a small shell in the Devonian becoming enormous in the Triassic. Certain species of sharks of medium size in the lower Eocene continue to increase till they attain the astounding dimensions in the Miocene and Pliocene of

5

over one hundred feet long. A certain fish appearing in the Devonian as a small fish of seven centimetres in length, becomes in the Carboniferous era a creature twenty seven centimetres in length. Among the mammals of Tertiary times this same law of steady increase in size has been operative, as seen in the Felidae, the stag, and the antelope. Man himself has, no doubt, been under the same law, and is probably a much larger animal than any of his Tertiary ancestors. In the vegetable world this process, in many cases, at least, has been reversed, and the huge treelike club-mosses and horsetails of Carboniferous times have dwindled in our time to very insignificant herbaceous forms.

Animals of overweening size are handicapped in many ways, so that nature in most cases finally abandons the gigantic and sticks to the medium and the small.

III

Can we fail to see the significance of the order in which life has appeared upon the globe—the ascending series from the simple to the more and more complex? Can we doubt that each series is the outcome of the one below it—that there is a logical sequence from the protozoa up through the invertebrates, the vertebrates, to man? Is it not like all that we know of the method of nature? Could we substitute the life of one period for that of another without doing obvious violence to the logic of nature? Is there no fundamental reason for the gradation we behold?

All animal life lowest in organization is earliest in time, and vice versa, the different classes of a sub-kingdom, and the different orders of a class, succeeding one another, as Cope says, in the relative order of their zoological rank. Thus the sponges are later than the protozoa, the corals succeed the sponges, the sea-urchins come after the corals, the shell-fish follow the sea-urchins, the articulates are later than the shell-fish, the vertebrates are later than the articulates. Among the former, the amphibian follows the fish, the reptile follows the amphibian, the mammal follows the reptile, and non-placental mammals are followed by the placental.

It almost seems as if nature hesitated whether to produce the mammal from the reptile or from the amphibian, as the mammal bears marks of both in its anatomy, and which was the parent stem is still a question.

The heart started as a simple tube in the Leptocardii; it divides itself into two cavities in the fishes, into three in the reptiles, and into four in the birds and mammals. So the ossification of the vertebral column takes place progressively, from the Silurian to the middle Jurassic.

The same ascending series of creation as a whole is repeated in the inception and development of every one of the higher animals to-day. Each one begins as a single cell, which soon becomes a congeries of cells, which is followed by congeries of congeries of cells, till the highly complex structure of the grown animal with all its intricate physiological activities and specialization of parts, is reached. It is typical of the course of the creative energy from the first unicellular life up to man, each succeeding stage flowing out of, and necessitated by, the preceding stage.

How slowly and surely the circulatory system improved! From the cold-blooded animal to the warm-blooded is a great advance. In the warm-blooded is developed the capacity to maintain a fixed temperature while that of the surrounding medium changes. The brain and nervous system display the same progressive ascent from the brainless acrania, up through the fishes, batrachia, reptiles, and birds to the top in mammals. The same with the skeletons in the invertebrates, from membrane to cartilage, from cartilage to bone, so that the primitive cartilage remaining in any part of the skeleton is considered a mark of inferiority.

According to Cope, there has been progressive improvement in the mechanism of the body—it has become a better and better machine. The suspension of the lower jaw, so as to bring the teeth nearer the power,—the masseter and related muscles,—was a slow evolution and a great advance. The fin is more primitive than the limb; the limbs themselves display a constantly increasing differentiation of parts from the batrachian to the mammalian. There was no good ankle joint in early Eocene times. The model ankle joint is a tongue and groove arrangement, and this is a later evolution. In Eocene times they were nearly all flat. The arched foot, too, comes in; this is an advance on the flat foot. The bones of the palms and soles are not locked until the later Tertiary. The vertebral column progressed in the same way, from flat to the double curve and the interlocking process, thus securing greatest strength with greatest mobility. In the earliest life locomotion was diffused, later it became concentrated. The worm walks with its whole body.

IV

If we figure to ourselves the geologic history of the earth under the symbol of a year of three hundred and sixty-five days, each day a million years, which is probably not far out of the way, then man, the biped, the Homo sapiens, in relation to this immense past, is of to-day, or of this very morning; while the origin of the first vertebrates, the fishes, from which he has arisen, falls nearer the middle of the great year. Or, dividing this geologic year into four divisions or seasons, primary, secondary, tertiary, and quaternary, the fishes fall in the primary, the reptiles in the secondary, the mammals in the tertiary, and man in the early quaternary.

If the fluid earth hardened, and the seas were formed in the first month of this year, then probably the first beginning of life appeared in the second month, the invertebrate in the third or fourth,—March or April,—the vertebrates in May or June, the amphibians in July or August, the reptiles in August or September, the mammals in October or November, and man in December,—separated from the first beginnings of life by all those millions upon millions of years.

If life is a ferment, as we are told it is, how long it took this yeast to leaven the whole loaf! Man is evidently the end of the series, he is the top of the biological tree. His specialization upon physical lines seems to have ended far back in geologic time; his future specialization and development is evidently to be upon mental and spiritual lines. Nature, as I have said, began to tend more and more to brains in the early Tertiary,—the autumn of the great year; her best harvest began to mature then, her grain began to ripen. Indeed, this increased cephalization of animal life in the fall of the great year does suggest a kind of ripening process, the turning of the sap and milk, which had been so abundant and so riotous in the earlier period, into fibre and fruit and seed.

May it not be that that long and sultry spring and summer of the earth's early history, a time probably longer than has since elapsed, played a part in the development of life analogous to that played by our spring and summer, making it opulent, varied, gigantic, and making possible the condensation and refinement that came with man in the recent period?

The earth is a pretty big apple, and the solar tree upon which it hangs is a pretty big tree, but why may it not have gone through a kind of ripening process for all that? its elements becoming less crude and acrid, and better suited to sustain the higher forms, as the eons passed?

At any rate, the results seem to justify such a fancy. The earth has slowly undergone a change that may fairly be called a ripening process; its soil has deepened and mellowed, its harsher features have softened, more and more color has come to its surface, the flowers have bloomed, the more succulent fruits have developed, the air has cleared, and love and benevolence and altruism have been born in the world.

V

Life had to creep or swim long before it could walk, and it walked long before it could fly; it had feeling long before it had eyes, and it no doubt had eyes long before it could hear or smell. It was capable of motion long before it had limbs; it assimilated food long before it had a mouth or a stomach. It had a digestive tract long before it had a spinal cord; it had nerve ganglia long before it had a well-defined brain. It had sensation long before it had perception; it was unisexual long before it was bisexual; it had a shell long before it had a skeleton; it had instinct and reflex action long before it had self-consciousness and reason. Always from the lower to the higher, from the simple to the more complex, and always slowly, gently.

Life has had its foetal stage, its stage of infancy, and childhood, and maturity, and will doubtless have its old age. It took it millions upon millions of years to get out of the sea upon dry land; and it took it more millions upon dry land, or since the Carboniferous age, when the air probably first began to be breathable,—all the vast stretch of the Secondary and Tertiary ages,—to get upright and develop a reasoning brain, and reach the estate of man. Step by step, in orderly succession, does creation move. In the rising and in the setting of the sun one may see how nature's great processes steal upon us, silently and unnoticed, yet always in sequence, stage succeeding stage, one thing following from another, the spectacular moment of sunset following inevitably from the quiet, unnoticed sinking of the sun in the west, or the startling flash of his rim above the eastern horizon only the fulfillment of the promise of the dawn. All is development and succession, and man is but the sunrise of the dawn of life in Cambrian or Silurian times, and is linked to that time as one hour of the day is linked to another.

The more complex life became, the more rapidly it seems to have developed, till it finally makes rapid strides to reach man. One seems to see Life, like a traveler on the road, going faster and faster as it nears its goal. Those long ages of unicellular life in the old seas, how immense they appear to have been; then how the age of invertebrates dragged on, millions upon millions of years; then the age of fishes; the Palaeozoic age, how vast—put by Haeckel at thirty-four millions of years, adding rock strata forty-one thousand feet thick; then the Mesozoic or third period, the age of reptiles, eleven million years, with strata twelve thousand feet thick. Then came the Caenozoic age, or age of mammals, three million years, with strata thirty-one hundred feet thick. The god of life was getting in a hurry now; man was not far off. A new device, the placenta, was hit upon in this age, and probably the diaphragm and the brain of animals, all greatly enlarged. Finally comes the Anthropozoic or Quaternary age, the age of man, three hundred thousand years, with not much addition to the sedimentary rocks.

Man seems to be the net result of it all, of all these vast cycles of Palaeozoic, Mesozoic, and Caenozoic life. He is the one drop finally distilled from the vast weltering sea of lower organic forms. It looks as if it all had to be before he could be—all the delay and waste and struggle and pain—all that long carnival of sea life, all that saturnalia of gigantic forms upon the land and in the air, all that rising and sinking of the continents, and all that shoveling to and fro and mixing of the soils, before the world was ready for him.

In the early Tertiary, millions of years ago, the earth seems to have been ripe for man. The fruits and vegetables and the forest trees were much as we know them, the animals that have been most serviceable to us were here, spring and summer and fall and winter came and went, evidently birds sang, insects hummed, flowers bloomed, fruits and grains and nuts ripened, and yet man as man was not.

Under the city of London is a vast deposit of clay in which thousands of specimens of fossil fruit have been found like our date, cocoanut, areca, custard-apple, gourd, melon, coffee, bean, pepper, and cotton plant, but no sign of man. Why was his development so tardy? What animal profited by this rich vegetable life? The hope and promise of the human species at that time probably slept in some lowly marsupial. Man has gathered up into himself, as he traveled his devious way, all the best powers of the animal kingdom he has passed through. His brain supplies him with all that his body lacks, and more. His specialization is in this highly developed organ. It is this that separates him so widely from all other animals.

Man has no wings, and yet he can soar above the clouds; he is not swift of foot, and yet he can out-speed the fleetest hound or horse; he has but feeble weapons in his organization, and yet he can slay or master all the great beasts; his eye is not so sharp as that of the eagle or the vulture, and yet he can see into the farthest depths of siderial space; he has only very feeble occult powers of communication with his fellows, and yet he can talk around the world and send his voice across mountains and deserts; his hands are weak things beside a lion's paw or an elephant's trunk, and yet he can move mountains and stay rivers and set bounds to the wildest seas. His dog can out-smell him and out-run him and out-bite him, and yet his dog looks up to him as to a god. He has erring reason in place of unerring instinct, and yet he has changed the face of the planet.

Without the specialization of the lower animals,—their wonderful adaptation to particular ends,—their tools, their weapons, their strength, their speed, man yet makes them all his servants. His brain is more than a match for all the special advantages nature has given them. The one gift of reason makes him supreme in the world.

VI

We have a stake in all the past life of the globe. It is no doubt a scientific fact that your existence and mine were involved in the first cell that appeared, that the first zoophyte furthered our fortunes, that the first worm gave us a lift. Great good luck came to us when the first pair of eyes were invented, probably by the trilobite back in Silurian times; when the first ear appeared, probably in Carboniferous times; when the first pair of lungs grew out of a fish's air-bladder, probably in Triassic times; when the first four-chambered heart was developed and double circulation established, probably with the first warm-blooded animal in Mesozoic times.

These humble forms started the brain, the nervous system, the circulation, sight, hearing, smell; they invented the liver, the kidneys, the lungs, the heart, the stomach, and led the way to every organ and power my body and mind have to-day. They were the pioneers, they were the dim remote forebears, they conserved and augmented the fund of life and passed it along.

All their struggles, their discipline, their battles, their failures, their successes, were for you and me. Man has had the experience of all the animals below him. He has suffered and struggled as a fish, he has groveled and devoured as a reptile, he has fought and triumphed as a quadruped, he has lived in trees as a monkey, he has inhabited caves with the wolf and the bear, he has roamed the forests and plains as a savage, he has survived without fire or clothes or weapons or tools, he has lived with the mastodon and all the saurian monsters, he has held his own against great odds, he has survived the long battles of the land and the sea, he weathered the ice-sheet that overrode both hemispheres, he has seen many forms become extinct. In the historic period he has survived plague and pestilence, and want and famine. What must he have survived in prehistoric times! What must he have had to contend with as a cave-dweller, as a tree-dweller, as a river-drift man! Before he had tools or weapons what must he have had to contend with!

Nature was full of sap and rioted in rude strength well up to Quaternary times, producing extravagant forms which apparently she had no use for, as she has discontinued them.

In all these things you and I had our part and lot; of this prodigal outpouring of life we have reaped the benefit; amid these bizarre forms and this carnival of lust and power, the manward impulse was nourished and forwarded. In Eocene times nearly half the mammals lived on other animals; it must have been an age of great slaughter. It favored the development of fleetness and cunning, in which we too have an interest. Our rude progenitor was surely there in some form, and escaped the slaughter. Then or later it is thought he took to the trees to escape his enemies, as the rats in Jamaica have taken to the trees to escape the mongoose. To his tree-climbing we probably owe our hand, with its opposing thumb.

In all his disguises he is still our ancestor. His story reads like a fairy book. Never did nimble fancy of childhood invent such transformations—only the transformations are so infinitely slow, and attended with such struggle and suffering. Strike out the element of time and we have before us a spectacle more novel and startling than any hocus-pocus or legerdemain that ever set the crowd agape.

In every form man has passed through, he left behind some old member or power and took on some new. He left his air-bladder and his gills and his fins with the fishes; he got his lungs from the dipnoans, the precursors of the amphibians, and from these last he got his four limbs; he left some part of his anatomy with the reptile, and took something in exchange, probably his flexible neck. Somewhere along his line he picked up the four-chambered heart, the warm blood, the placenta, the diaphragm, the plantigrade foot, the mammary glands—indeed, what has he not picked up on the long road of his many transformations? He left some of his superfluous forty-four teeth with his ancestral quadrumana of Eocene times, and kept thirty-two. He picked up his brain somewhere on the road, probably far back in Palaeozoic times, but how has he developed and enlarged it, till it is now the one supreme thing in the world! His fear, his cunning, his anger, his treachery, his hoggishness—all his animal passions—he brought with him from his animal ancestors; but his moral and spiritual nature, his altruism, his veneration, his religious emotions, his aesthetic perceptions—have come to him as a man, supplementing his lower nature, as it were, with another order of senses—a finer sight, a finer touch, wrought in him by the discipline of life, and the wonder of the world about him, beginning de novo in him only as the wing began de novo in the bird, or the color began de novo in the flower—struck out from preexisting potentialities. The father of the eye is the light, and the father of the ear is the vibration of the air, but the father of man's higher nature is a question of quite another sort. About the only thing in his physical make-up that man can call his own is his chin. None of the orders below him seem to have what can strictly be called a chin.

Man owes his five toes and five fingers to the early amphibians of the sub-carboniferous times. The first tangible evidence of these five toes upon the earth is, to me, very interesting. The earliest record of them that I have heard of is furnished by a slab of shale from Pennsylvania, upon which, while it was yet soft mud, our first five-toed ancestor had left the imprint of his four feet. He was evidently a small, short-legged gentleman with a stride of only about thirteen inches, and he carried a tail instead of a cane. He was probably taking a stroll upon the shores of that vast Mediterranean Sea that occupied all the interior of the continent when he crossed his mud flat. It was raining that morning—how many million years ago?—as we know from the imprint of the raindrops upon the mud. Probably the shower did not cause him to quicken his pace, as amphibians rather like the rain. Just what his immediate forbears were like, or what the forms were that connected him with the fishes, we shall probably never know. Doubtless the great book of the rocky strata somewhere holds the secret, if we are ever lucky enough to open it at the right place. How many other secrets, that evolutionists would like to know, those torn and crumpled leaves hold!

It is something to me to know that it rained that day when our amphibian ancestor ventured out. The weather was beginning to get organized also, and settling down to business. It had got beyond the state of perpetual mist and fog of the earlier ages, and the raindrops were playing their parts. Yet, from all the evidence we have, we infer that the climate was warm and very humid, like that of a greenhouse, and that vegetation, mostly giant ferns and rushes and lycopods, was very rank, but there was no grass, or moss, no deciduous trees, or flowers, or fruit, as we know these things.

A German anatomist says that we have the vestiges of one hundred and eighty organs which have stuck to us from our animal ancestors,—now useless, or often worse than useless, like the vermiform appendix. Eleven of these superannuated and obsolete organs we bring from the fishes, four from amphibians and reptiles. The external ear is a vestige—of no use any more. Our dread of snakes we no doubt inherited from our simian ancestors.

How life refined and humanized as time went on, sobered down and became more meditative, keeping step, no doubt, with the amelioration of the soil out of which all life finally comes. Life's bank account in the soil was constantly increasing; more and more of the inorganic was wrought up into the organic; the value of every clod underfoot was raised. The riot of gigantic forms ceased, and they became ashes. The giant and uncouth vegetation ceased, and left ashes or coal. The beech, the maple, the oak, the olive, the palm came in. The giant sea serpents disappeared; the horse, the ox, the swine, the dog, the quail, the dove came in. The placental mammals developed. The horse grew in size and beauty. When we first come upon his trail, he is a four-hoof-toed animal no larger than a fox. Later on we find him the size of a sheep with one of his toes gone; still later—many hundred thousand years, no doubt—we find him the size of a donkey, with still fewer toes, and so on till we reach the superb creature we know.

The creative energy seems to have worked in geologic time and in the geologic field just as it works here and now, in yonder vineyard or in yonder marsh,—blindly, experimentally, but persistently and successfully. The winged seeds find their proper soil, because they search in every direction; the climbing vines find their support, because in the same blind way they feel in all directions. Plants and animals and races of men grope their way to new fields, to new powers, to new inventions.

Indeed, how like an inventor Nature has worked, constantly improving her models, adding to and changing as experience would seem to dictate! She has developed her higher and more complex forms as man has developed his printing-press, or steam-engine, from rude, simple beginnings. From the two-chambered heart of the fish she made the treble-chambered heart of the frog, and then the four-chambered heart of the mammal. The first mammary gland had no nipples; the milk oozed out and was licked off by the young. The nipple was a great improvement, as was the power of suckling in the young.

Experimenting and experimenting endlessly, taking a forward step only when compelled by necessity,—this is the way of Nature,—experimenting with eyes, with ears, with teeth, with limbs, with feet, with toes, with wings, with bladders and lungs, with scales and armors, hitting upon the backbone only after long trials with other forms, hitting upon the movable eye only after long ages of other eyes, hitting on the mammal only after long ages of egg-laying vertebrates, hitting on the placenta only recently,—experimenting all around the circle, discarding and inventing, taking ages to perfect the nervous system, ages and ages to develop the centralized ganglia, the brain. First life was like a rabble, a mob, without thought or head, then slowly organization went on, as it were, from family to clan, from clan to tribe, from tribe to nation, or centralized government—the brain of man—all parts duly subordinated and directed,—millions of cells organized and working on different functions to one grand end,—cooperation, fraternization, division of labor, altruism, etc.

The cell was the first invention; it is the unit of life,—a speck of protoplasm with a nucleus. To educate this cell till it could combine with its fellows and form the higher animals seems to have been the aim of the creative energy. First the cell, then combinations of cells, then combinations of combinations, then more and more complex combinations till the body of man is reached, where endless confraternities of cells, all with different functions, working to build and sustain different organs,—brain, heart, liver, muscles, nerves,—yet all working together for one grand end—the body and mind of man. In their last analysis, all made up of the same cells—their combinations and organization making the different forms.

Evolution touches all forms but tarries with few. Many are called but few are chosen—chosen to lead the man-impulse upward. Myriads of forms are left behind, like driftwood caught in the eddies of a current. The clam has always remained a clam, the oyster remained an oyster. The cockroach is about the same creature to-day that it was untold aeons ago; so is the shark, and so are many other forms of marine life. Often where old species have gone out and new come in, no progress has been made.

Evolution concentrates along certain lines. The biological tree behaves like another tree, branches die and drop off (species become extinct), others mature and remain, while some central shoot pushes upward. Many of the huge reptilian and mammalian branches perished in comparatively late times.

As nothing is more evident than that the same measure of life or of vital energy—power of growth, power of resistance, power of reproduction—is not meted out equally to all the individuals of a species, or to all species, so it is evident that this power of progressive development is not meted out equally to all races of mankind, or to all of the individuals of the same race. The central impulse of development seems to have come from the East, in historic times at least, and to have followed the line of the Mediterranean, to have culminated in Europe. And this progress has certainly been the work of a few minds—minds exceptionally endowed.

For the most part the barbarian races do not progress. Their exceptional minds or characters do not lead the tribes to higher planes of thought, In all countries we still see these barbarous people which man in his progress has left behind. Our civilization is like a field of light that fades off into shadows and darkness. There is this margin of undeveloped humanity on all sides. Always has it been so in the animal life of the globe; the higher forms have been pushed up from the lower, and the lower have remained and continued to multiply unchanged.

It seems as if some central and cherished impulse had pushed on through each form, and by successive steps had climbed from height to height, gaining a little here and a little there, intensifying and concentrating as time went on, very vague and diffuse at first, embryonic so to speak, during the first half of the great geologic year, but quickening more and more, differentiating more and more, delayed and defeated many times, no doubt, yet never destroyed, leaving form after form unchanged behind it, till it at last reached its goal in man.

After evolution has done all it can do for us toward solving the mystery of creation, much remains unsolved.

Through evolution we see creation in travail-pains for millions of years to bring forth the varied forms of life as we know them; but the mystery of the inception of this life, and of the origin of the laws that have governed its development, remains. What lies back of it all? Who or what planted the germ of the biological tree, and predetermined all its branches? What determined one branch to eventuate in man, another in the dog, the horse, the bird, or the reptile?

From the finite or human point of view we feel compelled to say some vaster being or intelligence must have had the thought of all these things from the beginning or before the beginning.

It is quite impossible for me to believe that fortuitous variation—variation all around the circle— could have resulted in the evolution of man. There must have been a predetermined tendency to variation in certain directions. To introduce chance into the world is to introduce chaos. No more would the waters of the interiors of the continents find their way to the sea, were there not a slant in that direction, than could haphazard variation, though checked and controlled by natural selection, result in the production of the race of man. This view may be only the outcome of our inevitable anthropomorphism which we cannot escape from, no matter how deep we dive or high we soar.

II
THE DIVINE ABYSS
I

In making the journey to the great Southwest,—Colorado, New Mexico, and Arizona,—if one does not know his geology, he is pretty sure to wish he did, there is so much geology scattered over all these Southwestern landscapes, crying aloud to be read. The book of earthly revelation, as shown by the great science, lies wide open in that land, as it does in few other places on the globe. Its leaves fairly flutter in the wind, and the print is so large that he who runs on the California Limited may read it. Not being able to read it at all, or not taking any interest in it, is like going to Rome or Egypt or Jerusalem, knowing nothing of the history of those lands.

Of course, we have just as much geology in the East and Middle West, but the books are closed and sealed, as it were, by the enormous lapse of time since these portions of the continent became dry land. The eroding and degrading forces have ages since passed the meridian of their day's work, and grass and verdure hide their footsteps. But in the great West and Southwest, the gods of erosion and degradation seem yet in the heat and burden of the day's toil. Their unfinished landscapes meet the eye on every hand. Many of the mountains look as if they were blocked out but yesterday, and one sees vast naked flood-plains, and painted deserts and bad lands and dry lake-bottoms, that suggest a world yet in the making.

Some force has scalped the hills, ground the mountains, strangled the rivers, channeled the plains, laid bare the succession of geologic ages, stripping off formation after formation like a garment, or cutting away the strata over hundreds of square miles, as we pry a slab from a rock—and has done it all but yesterday. If we break the slab in the prying, and thus secure only part of it, leaving an abrupt jagged edge on the part that remains, we have still a better likeness of the work of these great geologic quarrymen. But other workmen, invisible to our eyes, have carved these jagged edges into novel and beautiful forms.

The East is old, old! the West, with the exception of the Rocky Mountains, is of yesterday in comparison. The Hudson was an ancient river before the Mississippi was born, and the Catskills were being slowly carved from a vast plateau while the rocks that were to form many of the Western ranges were being laid down as sediment in the bottom of the sea. California is yet in her teens, while New England in comparison is an octogenarian. Just as much geology in the East as in the West, did I say? Not as much visible geology, not as much by many chapters of earth history, not as much by all the later formations, by most of the Mesozoic and Tertiary deposits. The vast series of sedimentary rocks since the Carboniferous age, to say nothing of the volcanic, that make up these periods, are largely wanting east of the Mississippi, except in New Jersey and in some of the Gulf States. They are recent. They are like the history of our own period compared with that of Egypt and Judea. It is mainly these later formations— the Permian, the Jurassic, the Triassic, the Cretaceous, the Eocene,—that give the prevailing features to the South-western landscape that so astonish Eastern eyes. From them come most of the petrified remains of that great army of extinct reptiles and mammals—the three-toed horse, the sabre-toothed tiger, the brontosaurus, the fin-backed lizard, the imperial mammoth, the various dinosaurs, some of them

11

gigantic in form and fearful in aspect—that of late years have appeared in our museums and that throw so much light upon the history of the animal life of the globe. Most of the sedimentary rocks of New York and New England were laid down before these creatures existed.

Now I am not going to write an essay on the geology of the West, for I really have little first-hand knowledge upon that subject, but I would indicate the kind of interest in the country I was most conscious of during my recent trip to the Pacific Coast and beyond. Indeed, quite a geologic fever raged in me most of the time. The rocks attracted me more than the birds, the sculpturing of the landscapes engaged my attention more than the improvements of the farms—what Nature had done more than what man was doing. The purely scenic aspects of the country are certainly remarkable, and the human aspects interesting, but underneath these things, and striking through them, lies a vast world of time and change that to me is still more remarkable, and still more interesting. I could not look out of the car windows without seeing the spectre of geologic time stalking across the hills and plains.

As one leaves the prairie States and nears the great Southwest, he finds Nature in a new mood—she is dreaming of canyons; both cliffs and soil have canyon stamped upon them, so that your eye, if alert, is slowly prepared for the wonders of rock-carving it is to see on the Colorado. The canyon form seems inherent in soil and rock. The channels of the little streams are canyons, vertical sides of adobe soil, as deep as they are broad, rectangle grooves in the ground.

Through all this arid region nature is abrupt, angular, and sudden—the plain squarely abutting the cliff, the cliff walling the canon; the dry water-course sunk in the plain like a carpenter's groove into a plank. Cloud and sky look the same as at home, but the earth is a new earth—new geologically, and new in the lines of its landscapes. It seems by the forms she develops that Nature must use tools that she long since discarded in the East. She works as if with the square and the saw and the compass, and uses implements that cut like chisels and moulding-planes. Right lines, well-defined angles, and tablelike tops of buttes and mesas alternate with perfect curves, polished domes, carved needles, and fluted escarpments.

In the features of our older landscapes there is little or nothing that suggests architectural forms or engineering devices; in the Far West one sees such forms and devices everywhere.

In visiting the Petrified Forests in northern Arizona we stood on the edge of a great rolling plain and looked down upon a wide, deeply eroded stretch of country below us that suggested a vast army encampment, covered as it was with great dome-shaped, tent-like mounds of a light terra-cotta color, with open spaces like streets or avenues between them. There were hundreds or thousands of these earthy tents stretching away for twenty-five miles. Along the horizon was a gigantic stockade of red, rounded pillars, or a solid line of mosque-like temples. How unreal, how spectral it all seemed! Not a sound or sign of life in the whole painted solitude—a deserted camp, or one upon which the silence of death had fallen. Here, in Carboniferous times, grew the gigantic fern-like trees, the Sigillaria and Lepidodendron, whose petrified trunks, for aeons buried beneath the deposit of the Permian seas, and then, during other aeons, slowly uncovered by the gentle action of the eroding rains, we saw scattered on the ground.

You first see Nature beginning to form the canon habit in Colorado and making preliminary studies for her masterpiece, the Grand Canon. Huge square towers and truncated cones and needles and spires break the horizon-lines. Here all her water-courses, wet or dry, are deep grooves in the soil, with striking and pretty carvings and modelings adorning their vertical sides. In the railway cuts you see the same effects—miniature domes and turrets and other canon features carved out by the rains. The soil is massive and does not crumble like ours and seek the angle of repose; it gives way in masses like a brick wall. It is architectural soil, it seeks approximately the right angle—the level plain or the vertical wall. It erodes easily under running water, but it does not slide; sand and clay are in such proportions as to make a brittle but not a friable soil.

Before you are out of Colorado, you begin to see these novel architectural features on the horizon-line—the canon turned bottom side up, as it were. In New Mexico, the canon habit of the erosion forces is still more pronounced. The mountain-lines are often as architectural in the distance, or arbitrary, as the sky-line of a city. You may see what you half persuade yourself is a huge brick building notching the horizon,—an asylum, a seminary, a hotel,—but it is only a fragment of red sandstone, carved out by wind and rain.

Presently the high colors of the rocks appear—high cliffs with terra-cotta facades, and a new look in the texture of the rocks, a soft, beaming, less frowning expression, and colored as if by the Western sunsets. We are looking upon much younger rocks geologically than we see at home, and they have the tints and texture of youth. The landscape and the mountains look young, because they look unfinished, like a house half up. The workmen have but just knocked off work to go to dinner; their great trenches, their freshly opened quarries, their huge dumps, their foundations, their cyclopean masonry, their half-finished structures breaking the horizon-lines, their square gashes through the mountains,—all impress the eyes of a traveler from the eastern part of the continent, where the earth-building and earth-carving forces finished their work ages ago.

II

Hence it is that when one reaches the Grand canon of the Colorado, if he has kept his eyes and mind open, he is prepared to see striking and unusual things. But he cannot be fully prepared for just what he does see, no matter how many pictures of it he may have seen, or how many descriptions of it he may have read.

A friend of mine who took a lively interest in my Western trip wrote me that he wished he could have been present with his kodak when we first looked upon the Grand Canon. Did he think he could have got a picture of our souls? His camera would have shown him only our silent, motionless forms as we stood transfixed by that first view of the stupendous spectacle. Words do not come readily to one's lips, or gestures to one's body, in the presence of such a scene. One of my companions said that the first thing that came into her mind was the old text, "Be still, and know that I am God." To be still on such an occasion is the easiest thing in the world, and to feel the surge of solemn and reverential emotions is equally easy; is, indeed, almost inevitable. The immensity of the scene, its tranquillity, its order, its strange, new beauty, and the monumental character of its many forms—all these tend to beget in the beholder an attitude of silent wonder and solemn admiration. I wished at the moment that we might have been alone with the glorious spectacle,—that we had hit upon an hour when the public had gone to dinner. The smoking and joking tourists sauntering along in apparent indifference, or sitting with their backs to the great geologic drama, annoyed me. I pity the person who can gaze upon the spectacle unmoved. Some are actually terrified by it. I was told of a strong man, an eminent lawyer from a Western city, who literally fell to the earth at the first view, and could not again be induced to look upon it. I saw a woman prone upon the ground near the brink at Hopi Point, weeping silently and long; but from what she afterward told me I know it was not from terror or sorrow, but from the overpowering gladness of the ineffable beauty and harmony of the scene. It moved her like the grandest music. Her inebriate soul could find relief only in tears.

Harriet Monroe was so wrought up by the first view that she says she had to fight against the desperate temptation to fling herself down into the soft abyss, and thus redeem the affront which the very beating of her heart had offered to the inviolable solitude. Charles Dudley Warner said of it, "I experienced for a moment an indescribable terror of nature, a confusion of mind, a fear to be alone in such a presence."

It is beautiful, oh, how beautiful! but it is a beauty that awakens a feeling of solemnity and awe. We call it the "Divine Abyss." It seems as much of heaven as of earth. Of the many descriptions of it, none seems adequate. To rave over it, or to pour into it a torrent of superlatives, is of little avail. My companion came nearer the mark when she quietly repeated from Revelation, "And he carried me away in the spirit to a great and high mountain, and shewed me that great city, the holy Jerusalem." It does, indeed, suggest a far-off, half-sacred antiquity, some greater Jerusalem, Egypt, Babylon, or India. We speak of it as a scene: it is more like a vision, so foreign is it to all other terrestrial spectacles, and so surpassingly beautiful.

To ordinary folk the sight is so extraordinary, so unlike everything one's experience has yielded, and so unlike the results of the usual haphazard working of the blind forces of nature, that I did not wonder when people whom I met on the rim asked me what I supposed did all this. I could even sympathize with the remark of an old woman visitor who is reported to have said that she thought they had built the canon too near the hotel. The enormous cleavage which the canon shows, the abrupt drop from the brink of thousands of feet, the sheer faces of perpendicular walls of dizzy height, give at first the impression that it is all the work of some titanic quarryman, who must have removed cubic miles of strata as we remove cubic yards of earth. Go out to Hopi Point or O'Neil's Point, and, as you emerge from the woods, you get a glimpse of a blue or rose-purple gulf opening before you. The solid ground ceases suddenly, and an aerial perspective, vast and alluring, takes its place; another heaven, countersunk in the earth, transfixes you on the brink. "Great God!" I can fancy the first beholder of it saying, "what is this? Do I behold the transfiguration of the earth? Has the solid ground melted into thin air? Is there a firmament below as well as above? Has the earth veil at last been torn aside, and the red heart of the globe been laid bare?" If this first witness was not at once overcome by the beauty of the earthly revelation before him, or terrified by its strangeness and power, he must have stood long, awed, spellbound, speechless with astonishment, and thrilled with delight. He may have seen vast and glorious prospects from mountaintops, he may have looked down upon the earth and seen it unroll like a map before him; but he had never before looked into the earth as through a mighty window or open door, and beheld

13

depths and gulfs of space, with their atmospheric veils and illusions and vast perspectives, such as he had seen from mountain-summits, but with a wealth of color and a suggestion of architectural and monumental remains, and a strange, almost unearthly beauty, such as no mountain-view could ever have afforded him. Three features of the canon strike one at once: its unparalleled magnitude, its architectural forms and suggestions, and its opulence of color effects—a chasm nearly a mile deep and from ten to twenty miles wide, in which Niagara would be only as a picture upon your walls, in which the Pyramids, seen from the rim, would appear only like large tents, in which the largest building upon the earth would dwindle to insignificant proportions. There are amphitheatres and mighty aisles eight miles long and three or four miles wide and three or four thousand feet deep. There are room-like spaces eight hundred feet high; there are well-defined alcoves with openings a mile wide; there are niches six hundred feet high overhung by arched lintels; there are pinnacles and rude statues from one hundred to two hundred feet high. Here I am running at once into allusions to the architectural features and suggestions of the canon, which must play a prominent part in all faithful attempts to describe it. There are huge, truncated towers, vast, horizontal mouldings; there is the semblance of balustrades on the summit of a noble facade. In one of the immense halls we saw, on an elevated platform, the outlines of three enormous chairs, fifty feet or more high, and behind and above them the suggestion of three more chairs in partial ruin. Indeed, there is such an opulence of architectural forms in this divine abyss as one has never before dreamed of seeing wrought by the blind forces of nature. These forces have here foreshadowed all the noblest architecture of the world. Many of the vast carved and ornamental masses which diversify the canon have been fitly named temples, as Shiva's Temple, a mile high, carved out of the red Carboniferous limestone, and remarkably symmetrical in its outlines. Near it is the Temple of Isis, the Temple of Osiris, the Buddha Temple, the Horus Temple, and the Pyramid of Cheops. Farther to the east is the Diva Temple, the Brahma Temple, the Temple of Zoroaster, and the Tomb of Odin. Indeed, everywhere are there suggestions of temples and tombs, pagodas and pyramids, on a scale that no work of human hands can rival. "The grandest objects," says Major Dutton, "are merged in a congregation of others equally grand." With the wealth of form goes a wealth of color. Never, I venture to say, were reds and browns and grays and vermilions more appealing to the eye than they are as they softly glow in this great canyon. The color-scheme runs from the dark, sombre hue of the gneiss at the bottom, up through the yellowish brown of the Cambrian layers, and on up through seven or eight broad bands of varying tints of red and vermilion, to the broad yellowish-gray at the top.

III

The north side of the canyon has been much more deeply and elaborately carved than the south side; most of the great architectural features are on the north side—the huge temples and fortresses and amphitheatres. The strata dip very gently to the north and northeast, while the slope of the surface is to the south and southeast. This has caused the drainage from the great northern plateaus to flow into the canyon and thus cut and carve the north side as we behold it.

The visitor standing upon the south side looks across the great chasm upon the bewildering maze of monumental forms, some of them as suggestive of human workmanship as anything in nature well can be, —crumbling turrets and foundations, forms as distinctly square as any work of man's hands, vast fortress-like structures with salients and entering angles and wing walls resisting the siege of time, huge pyramidal piles rising story on story, three thousand feet or more above their foundations, each successive story or superstructure faced by a huge vertical wall which rises from a sloping talus that connects it with the story next below. The slopes or taluses represent the softer rock, the vertical walls the harder layers. Usually four or five of these receding stories make up each temple or pyramid. Some of the larger structures show all the strata from the cap of light Carboniferous limestone at the top to the gray Cambrian sandstone at the bottom. From others, such as the Temple of Isis, all the upper formations are gone with a pile of disintegrated red sandstone, like a mass of brick dust on the top where the fragment of the old red wall made its last stand. In those masses, which are still crowned with the light gray limestone, one sees how surely the process of disintegration is going on by the fragments and debris of light gray rock, like the chips of giant workmen, that strew the deeper-colored slopes below them. These fragments fade out as the eye drops down the slopes, as if they had melted like bits of ice. Indeed, the melting of ice and the dissolution of a rock do not differ much except that one is very rapid and the other infinitely slow. In time (not man's time, but the Lord's time), all these light masses that cap the huge temples will be weathered away, yea, and all the vast red layers beneath them, and the huge structures will be slowly consumed by time. The Colorado River will carry their ashes to the sea, and where they once stood will be seen gray, desert-like plateaus. Their outlines now stand out like skeletons from which the flesh has been removed—sharp, angular, obtrusive, but bound together as by ligaments of granite. The tooth of time gnaws at them day and night and has been gnawing for thousands of centuries, so that in some cases only

14

their stumps remain. From the Temple of Isis and the Tomb of Odin the two or three upper stories are gone.

On the next page is the ground plan of the Temple of Isis, about twenty-five hundred feet high. The first story is about a thousand feet; the second, three hundred and fifty feet; the third, one hundred and fifty feet; the fourth, five hundred feet; and the fifth, five hundred feet. The finish at the top shows as a heavy crumbling wall, probably one hundred feet or more high. How the mass seems to be resisting the siege of time, throwing out its salients here and there, and meeting the onset of the foes like a military engineer.

The pyramidal form of these rock-masses is accounted for by the fact that they were carved out from the top downward, and that each successive story is vastly older than the one immediately beneath it. The erosive forces have been working whole geologic ages longer on the top layer of rock than on the bottom layer; hence the topmost ones are entirely gone or else reduced to small dimensions. But what feature or quality of the rock it is that lends itself so readily or so inevitably to these architectural forms— the four square foundations, the end pilasters and balustrades, and so on—is to me not so clear. The peculiar rectangular jointings, the alternation of soft and hard layers, the nearly horizontal strata, and other things, no doubt, enter into the problem. Many of these features are found in our older geology of the East, as in the Catskills —horizontal strata, hard and soft layers alternating, but with the vertical jointing less pronounced; hence the Catskills have few canon-like valleys, though there are here and there huge gashes through the mountains that give a canon effect, and there are gigantic walls high up on the face of some of the mountains that suggest one side of a mighty canon. In the climate of the Catskills the rock-masses of the Colorado would crumble much more rapidly than they do here. The lines of many of these natural temples or fortresses are still more lengthened and attenuated than those of the Temple of Isis, appearing like mere skeletons of their former selves. The forms that weather out the formation above this, the Permian, appear to be more rotund, and tend more to domes and rounded hills.

One of the most surprising features of the Grand canon is its cleanness—its freedom from debris. It is a home of the gods, swept and garnished; no litter or confusion or fragments of fallen and broken rocky walls anywhere. Those vast sloping taluses are as clean as a meadow; rarely at the foot of the huge vertical walls do you see a fragment of fallen rock. It is as if the processes of erosion and degradation were as gentle as the dews and the snows, and carved out this mighty abyss grain by grain, which has probably been the case. That much of this red sandstone, from the amount of iron it contains, or from some other cause, disintegrates easily and rapidly, is very obvious. Looking down from Hopi Point upon a vast ridge called the "Man-of-War," one sees on the top, where once there must have been a huge wall of rock, a long level area of red soil that suggests a garden, the more so because it is regularly divided up into sections by straight lines of huge stone placed as if by the hands of man.

One's sense of the depths of the canyon is so great that it almost makes one dizzy to see the little birds fly out over it, or plunge down into it. One seems to fear that they too will get dizzy and fall to the bottom. We watched a line of tourists on mules creeping along the trail across the inner plateau, and the unaided eye had trouble to hold them; they looked like little red ants. The eye has more difficulty in estimating sizes and distances beneath it than when they are above or on a level with it, because it is so much less familiar with depth than with height or lateral dimensions.

Another remarkable and unexpected feature of the canyon is its look of ordered strength. Nearly all the lines are lines of greatest strength. The prevailing profile line everywhere is that shown herewith. The upright lines represent lines of cyclopean masonry, and the slant is the talus that connects them, covered with a short, sage-colored growth of some kind, and as soft to the eye as the turf of our fields. The simple, strong structural lines assert themselves everywhere, and give that look of repose and security characteristic of the scene. The rocky forces always seem to retreat in good order before the onslaught of time; there is neither rout nor confusion; everywhere they present a calm upright front to the foe. And the fallen from their ranks, where are they? A cleaner battlefield between the forces of nature one rarely sees.

The weaker portions are, of course, constantly giving way. The elements incessantly lay siege to these fortresses and take advantage of every flaw or unguarded point, so that what stands has been seven times, yea, seventy times seven times tested, and hence gives the impression of impregnable strength. The angles and curves, the terraces and foundations, seem to be the work of some master engineer, with only here and there a toppling rock.

I was puzzled to explain to myself the reason of a certain friendly and familiar look which the great abyss had for me. One sees or feels at a glance that it was not born of the throes and convulsions of nature—of earthquake shock or volcanic explosion. It does not suggest the crush of matter and the wreck of worlds. Clearly it is the work of the more gentle and beneficent forces. This probably accounts for the friendly look. Some of the inner slopes and plateaus seemed like familiar ground to me: I must have played upon them when a school-boy. Bright Angel Creek, for some inexplicable reason, recalled a favorite trout-stream of my native hills, and the old Cambrian plateau that edges the inner chasm, as we looked down upon it from nearly four thousand feet above, looked like the brown meadow where we played ball in the old school-days, friendly, tender, familiar, in its slopes and terraces, in its tints and basking sunshine, but grand and awe-inspiring in its depths, its huge walls, and its terrific precipices.

The geologists are agreed that the canyon is only of yesterday in geologic time,—the Middle Tertiary,—and yet behold the duration of that yesterday as here revealed, probably a million years or more! We can no more form any conception of such time than we can of the size of the sun or of the distance of the fixed stars.

The forces that did all this vast delving and sculpturing—the air, the rains, the frost, the sunshine—are as active now as they ever were; but their activity is a kind of slumbering that rarely makes a sign. Only at long intervals is the silence of any part of the profound abyss broken by the fall of loosened rocks or sliding talus. We ourselves saw where a huge splinter of rock had recently dropped from the face of the cliff. In time these loosened masses disappear, as if they melted like ice. A city not made with hands, but as surely not eternal in the earth! In our humid and severe Eastern climate, frost and ice and heavy rains working together, all these architectural forms would have crumbled long ago, and fertile fields or hill-slopes would have taken their place. In the older Hawaiian Islands, which probably also date from Tertiary times, the rains have carved enormous canons and amphitheatres out of the hard volcanic rock, in some places grinding the mountains to such a thin edge that a man may literally sit astride them, each leg pointing into opposite valleys. In the next geologic age, the temples and monuments of the Grand Canon will have largely disappeared, and the stupendous spectacle will be mainly a thing of the past.

It seems to take millions of years to tame a mountain, to curb its rude, savage power, to soften its outlines, and bring fertility out of the elemental crudeness and barrenness. But time and the gentle rains of heaven will do it, as they have done it in the East, and as they are fast doing it in the West.

An old guide with whom I talked, who had lived in and about the canon for twenty-six years, said, "While we have been sitting here, the canon has widened and deepened"; which was, of course, the literal truth, the mathematical truth, but the widening and deepening could not have been apprehended by human sense.

Our little span of human life is far too narrow for us to be a witness of any of the great earth changes. These changes are so slow,—oh, so slow,—and human history is so brief. So far as we are concerned, the gods of the earth sit in council behind closed doors. All the profound, formative, world-shaping forces of nature go on in a realm that we can reach only through our imaginations. They so far transcend our human experiences that it requires an act of faith to apprehend them. The repose of the hills and the mountains, how profound! yet they may be rising or sinking before our very eyes, and we detect no sign. Only on exceptional occasions, during earthquakes or volcanic eruptions, is their dreamless slumber rudely disturbed.

Geologists tell us that from the great plateau in which the Grand Canon is cut, layers of rock many thousands of feet thick were cut away before the canon was begun.

Starting from the high plateau of Utah, and going south toward the canon, we descend a grand geologic stairway, every shelf or tread of which consists of different formations fifty or more miles broad, from the Eocene, at an altitude of over ten thousand feet at the start, across the Cretaceous, the Jurassic, the Triassic, the Permian, to the Carboniferous, which is the bottom or landing of the Grand Canon plateau at an altitude of about five thousand feet. Each step terminates more or less abruptly, the first by a drop of eight hundred feet, ornamented by rows of square obelisks and pilasters of uniform pattern and dimension, "giving the effect," says Major Dutton, "of a gigantic colonnade from which the entablature has been removed or has fallen in ruins."

The next step, or platform, the Cretaceous, slopes down gradually or dies out on the step beneath it; then comes the Jurassic, which ends in white sandstone cliffs several hundred feet high; then the Triassic, which ends in the famous vermilion cliffs thousands of feet high, most striking in color and in form; then the Permian tread, which also ends in striking cliffs, with their own style of color and architecture; and, lastly, the great Carboniferous platform in which the canon itself is carved. Now, all these various strata above the canon, making at one time a thickness of over a mile, were worn away in Pliocene times, before the cutting of the Grand Canon began. Had they remained, and been cut through, we should have had a chasm two miles deep instead of one mile.

The cutting power of a large, rapid volume of water, like the Colorado, charged with sand and gravel, is very great. According to Major Dutton, in the hydraulic mines of California, the escaping water has been known to cut a chasm from twelve to twenty feet deep in hard basaltic rock, in a single year. This is, of course, exceptional, but there have, no doubt, been times when the Colorado cut downward very rapidly. The enormous weathering of its side walls is to me the more wonderful, probably because the forces that have achieved this task are silent and invisible, and, so far as our experience goes, so infinitely slow in their action. The river is a tremendous machine for grinding and sawing and transporting, but the rains and the frost and the air and the sunbeams smite the rocks as with weapons of down, and one is naturally incredulous as to their destructive effects.

Some of the smaller rivers in the plateau region flow in very deep but very narrow canons. The rocks being harder and more homogeneous, the weathering has been slight. The meteoric forces have not taken a hand in the game. Thus the Parunuweap Canon is only twenty to thirty feet wide, but from six hundred to fifteen hundred feet deep.

I suppose the slow, inappreciable erosion to which the old guide alluded would have cut the canon since Middle Tertiary times. The river, eating downward at the rate of one sixteenth of an inch a year, would do it in about one million years. At half that rate it would do it in double that time. In the earlier part of its history, when the rainfall was doubtless greater, and the river fuller, the erosion must have been much more rapid than it is at present. The widening of the canon was doubtless a slower process than the downward cutting. But, as I have said, the downward cutting would tend to check itself from age to age, while the widening process would go steadily forward. Hence, when we look into the great abyss, we have only to remember the enormous length of time that the aerial and subaerial forces have been at work to account for it.

Two forces, or kinds of forces, have worked together in excavating the canon: the river, which is the primary factor, and the meteoric forces, which may be called the secondary, as they follow in the wake of the former. The river starts the gash downward, then the aerial forces begin to eat into the sides. Acting alone, the river would cut a trench its own width, and were the rocks through which it saws one homogeneous mass, or of uniform texture and hardness, the width of the trench would probably have been very uniform and much less than it is now. The condition that has contributed to its great width is the heterogeneity of the different formations—some hard and some soft. The softer bands, of course, introduce the element of weakness. They decay and crumble the more rapidly, and thus undermine the harder bands overlying them, which, by reason of their vertical fractures, break off and fall to the bottom, where they are exposed to the action of floods and are sooner or later ground up in the river's powerful maw. Hence the recession of the banks of the canon has gone steadily on with the downward cutting of the river. Where the rock is homogeneous, as it is in the inner chasm of the dark gneiss, the widening process seems to have gone on much more slowly. Geologists account for the great width of the main chasm when compared with the depth, on the theory that the forces that work laterally have been more continuously active than has the force that cuts downward. There is convincing evidence that the whole region has been many times lifted up since the cutting began, so that the river has had its active and passive stages. As its channel approached the sea level, its current would be much less rapid, and the downward cutting would practically cease, till the section was elevated again. But all the time the forces working laterally would be at work without interruption, and would thus gain on their checked brethren of the river bottom.

There is probably another explanation of what we see here. Apart from the mechanical weathering of the rocks as a result of the arid climate, wherein rapid and often extreme changes of temperature take place, causing the surface of the rocks to flake or scale off, there has doubtless been unusual chemical weathering, and this has been largely brought about by the element of iron that all these rocks possess. Their many brilliant colors are imparted to them by the various compounds of iron which enter into their composition. And iron, though the symbol of hardness and strength, is an element of weakness in rocks, as it causes them to oxidize or disintegrate more rapidly. In the marble canon, where apparently the rock contains no iron, the lateral erosion has been very little, though the river has cut a trench as deep as it has in other parts of its course.

How often I thought during those days at the canon of the geology of my native hills amid the Catskills, which show the effects of denudation as much older than that shown here as this is older than the washout in the road by this morning's shower! The old red sandstone in which I hoed corn as a farm-boy dates back to Middle Palaeozoic time, or to the spring of the great geologic year, while the canon is of the late autumn. Could my native hills have replied to my mute questionings, they would have said: "We were old, old, and had passed through the canon stage long before the Grand Canon was born. We have had all that experience, and have forgotten it ages ago. No vestiges of our canons remain. They have all been worn down and obliterated by the strokes of a hand as gentle as that of a passing cloud. Where they were, are now broad, fertile valleys, with rounded knolls and gentle slopes, and the sound of peaceful husbandry. The great ice sheet rubbed us and ploughed us, but our contours were gentle and rounded aeons before that event. When the Grand Canon is as old as we are, all its superb architectural features will have long since disappeared, its gigantic walls will have crumbled, and rolling plains and gentle valleys will have taken its place." All of which seems quite probable. With time enough, the gentle forces of air and water will surely change the whole aspect of this tremendous chasm.

On the second day we made the descent into the canon on mule-back. There is always satisfaction in going to the bottom of things. Then we wanted to get on more intimate terms with the great abyss, to wrestle with it, if need be, and to feel its power, as well as to behold it. It is not best always to dwell upon the rim of things or to look down upon them from afar. The summits are good, but the valleys have their charm, also; even the valley of humiliation has its lessons. At any rate, four of us were unanimous in our desire to sound that vast profound on mule-back, trusting that the return trip would satisfy our "climbing" aspirations, as it did.

It is quite worth while to go down into the canon on mule-back, if only to fall in love with a mule, and to learn what a sure-footed, careful, and docile creature, when he is on his good behavior, a mule can be. My mule was named "Johnny," and there was soon a good understanding between us. I quickly learned to turn the whole problem of that perilous descent over to him. He knew how to take the sharp turns and narrow shelves of that steep zigzag much better than I did. I do not fancy that the thought of my safety was "Johnny's" guiding star; his solicitude struck nearer home than that. There was much ice and snow on the upper part of the trail, and only those slender little legs of "Johnny's" stood between me and a tumble of two or three thousand feet. How cautiously he felt his way with his round little feet, as, with lowered head, he seemed to be scanning the trail critically! Only when he swung around the sharp elbows of the trail did his forefeet come near the edge of the brink. Only once or twice at such times, as we hung for a breath above the terrible incline, did I feel a slight shudder. One of my companions, who had never before been upon an animal's back, so fell in love with her "Sandy" that she longed for a trunk big enough in which to take him home with her.

It was more than worth while to make the descent to traverse that Cambrian plateau, which from the rim is seen to flow out from the base of the enormous cliffs to the brink of the inner chasm, looking like some soft, lavender-colored carpet or rug. I had never seen the Cambrian rocks, the lowest of the stratified formations, nor set my foot upon Cambrian soil. Hence a new experience was promised me. Rocky layers probably two or three miles thick had been worn away from the old Cambrian foundations, and when I looked down upon that gently undulating plateau, the thought of the eternity of time which it represented tended quite as much to make me dizzy as did the drop of nearly four thousand feet. We found it gravelly and desert-like, covered with cacti, low sagebrush, and other growths. The dim trail led us to its edge, where we could look down into the twelve-hundred-foot V-shaped gash which the river had cut into the dark, crude-looking Archaean rock. How distinctly it looked like a new day in creation where the horizontal, yellowish-gray beds of the Cambrian were laid down upon the dark, amorphous, and twisted older granite! How carefully the level strata had been fitted to the shapeless mass beneath it! It all looked like the work of a master mason; apparently you could put the point of your knife where one ended and the other began. The older rock suggested chaos and turmoil; the other suggested order and plan, as if the builder had said, "Now upon this foundation we will build our house." It is an interesting fact, the full geologic significance of which I suppose I do not appreciate, that the different formations are usually marked off from one another in just this sharp way, as if each one was, indeed, the work of a separate day of creation. Nature appears at long intervals to turn over a new leaf and start a new chapter in her great book. The transition from one geologic age to another appears to be abrupt: new colors, new constituents, new qualities appear in the rocks with a suddenness hard to reconcile with Lyell's doctrine of uniformitarianism, just as new species appear in the life of the globe with an abruptness hard to reconcile with Darwin's slow process of natural selection. Is sudden mutation, after all, the key to all these phenomena?

We ate our lunch on the old Cambrian table, placed there for us so long ago, and gazed down upon the turbulent river hiding and reappearing in its labyrinthian channel so far below us. It is worth while to make the descent in order to look upon the river which has been the chief quarryman in excavating the canon, and to find how inadequate it looks for the work ascribed to it. Viewed from where we sat, I judged it to be forty or fifty feet broad, but I was assured that it was between two and three hundred feet. Water and sand are ever symbols of instability and inconstancy, but let them work together, and they saw through mountains, and undermine the foundations of the hills.

It is always worth while to sit or kneel at the feet of grandeur, to look up into the placid faces of the earth gods and feel their power, and the tourist who goes down into the canon certainly has this privilege. We did not bring back in our hands, or in our hats, the glory that had lured us from the top, but we seemed to have been nearer its sources, and to have brought back a deepened sense of the magnitude of the forms, and of the depth of the chasm which we had heretofore gazed upon from a distance. Also we had plucked the flower of safety from the nettle danger, always an exhilarating enterprise.

In climbing back, my eye, now sharpened by my geologic reading, dwelt frequently and long upon the horizon where that cross-bedded Carboniferous sandstone joins the Carboniferous limestone above it. How much older the sandstone looked! I could not avoid the impression that its surface must have formed a plane of erosion ages and ages before the limestone had been laid down upon it.

We had left plenty of ice and snow at the top, but in the bottom we found the early spring flowers blooming, and a settler at what is called the Indian Gardens was planting his garden. Here I heard the song of the canon wren, a new and very pleasing bird-song to me. I think our dreams were somewhat disturbed that night by the impressions of the day, but our day-dreams since that time have at least been sweeter and more comforting, and I am sure that the remainder of our lives will be the richer for our having seen the Grand Canon.

III

THE SPELL OF THE YOSEMITE

I

Yosemite won my heart at once, as it seems to win the hearts of all who visit it. In my case many things helped to do it, but I am sure a robin, the first I had seen since leaving home, did his part. He struck the right note, he brought the scene home to me, he supplied the link of association. There he was, running over the grass or perching on the fence, or singing from a tree-top in the old familiar way. Where the robin is at home, there at home am I. But many other things helped to win my heart to the Yosemite—the whole character of the scene, not only its beauty and sublimity, but the air of peace and protection, and of homelike seclusion that pervades it; the charm of a nook, a retreat, combined with the power and grandeur of nature in her sternest moods.

After passing from the hotel at El Portal along the foaming and roaring Merced River, and amid the tumbled confusion of enormous granite boulders shaken down from the cliffs above, you cross the threshold of the great valley as into some vast house or hall carved out of the mountains, and at once feel the spell of the brooding calm and sheltered seclusion that pervades it. You pass suddenly from the tumultuous, the chaotic, into the ordered, the tranquil, the restful, which seems enhanced by the power and grandeur that encompass them about. You can hardly be prepared for the hush that suddenly falls upon the river and for the gentle rural and sylvan character of much that surrounds you; the peace of the fields, the seclusion of the woods, the privacy of sunny glades, the enchantment of falls and lucid waters, with a touch of human occupancy here and there—all this, set in that enormous granite frame, three or four thousand feet high, ornamented with domes and spires and peaks still higher,—it is all this that wins your heart and fills your imagination in the Yosemite.

As you ride or walk along the winding road up the level valley amid the noble pines and spruces and oaks, and past the groves and bits of meadow and the camps of many tents, and the huge mossy granite boulders here and there reposing in the shade of the trees, with the full, clear, silent river winding through the plain near you, you are all the time aware of those huge vertical walls, their faces scarred and niched, streaked with color, or glistening with moisture, and animated with waterfalls, rising up on either hand, thousands of feet high, not architectural, or like something builded, but like the sides and the four corners of the globe itself. What an impression of mass and of power and of grandeur in repose filters into you as you walk along! El Capitan stands there showing its simple sweeping lines through the trees as you approach, like one of the veritable pillars of the firmament. How long we are nearing it and passing it! It is so colossal that it seems near while it is yet far off. It is so simple that the eye takes in its naked grandeur at a glance. It demands of you a new standard of size which you cannot at once produce. It is as clean and smooth as the flank of a horse, and as poised and calm as a Greek statue. It curves out toward the base as if planted there to resist the pressure of worlds—probably the most majestic single granite column or mountain buttress on the earth. Its summit is over three thousand feet above you. Across the valley, nearly opposite, rise the Cathedral Rocks to nearly the same height, while farther along, beyond El Capitan, the Three Brothers shoulder the sky at about the same dizzy height. Near the head of the great valley, North Dome, perfect in outline as if turned in a lathe, and its brother, the Half Dome (or shall we say half-brother?) across the valley, look down upon Mirror Lake from an altitude of over four thousand feet. These domes suggest enormous granite bubbles if such were possible pushed up from below and retaining their forms through the vast geologic ages. Of course they must have weathered enormously, but as the rock seems to peel off in concentric sheets, their forms are preserved.

II

One warm, bright Sunday near the end of April, six of us walked up from the hotel to Vernal and Nevada Falls, or as near to them as we could get, and took our fill of the tumult of foaming waters

19

struggling with the wreck of huge granite cliffs: so impassive and immobile the rocks, so impetuous and reckless and determined the onset of the waters, till the falls are reached, when the obstructed river seems to find the escape and the freedom it was so eagerly seeking. Better to be completely changed into foam and spray by one single leap of six hundred feet into empty space, the river seems to say, than be forever baffled and tortured and torn on this rack of merciless boulders.

We followed the zigzagging trail up the steep side of the valley, touching melting snow banks in its upper courses, passing huge granite rocks also melting in the slow heat of the geologic ages, pausing to take in the rugged, shaggy spruces and pines that sentineled the mountain-sides here and there, or resting our eyes upon Liberty Cap, which carries its suggestive form a thousand feet or more above the Nevada Fall. What beauty, what grandeur attended us that day! the wild tumult of waters, the snow-white falls, the motionless avalanches of granite rocks, and the naked granite shaft, Liberty Cap, dominating all!

And that night, too, when we sat around a big camp-fire near our tents in the valley, and saw the full moon come up and look down upon us from behind Sentinel Rock, and heard the intermittent booming of Yosemite Falls sifting through the spruce trees that towered around us, and felt the tender, brooding spirit of the great valley, itself touched to lyric intensity by the grandeurs on every hand, steal in upon us, and possess our souls—surely that was a night none of us can ever forget. As Yosemite can stand the broad, searching light of midday and not be cheapened, so its enchantments can stand the light of the moon and the stars and not be rendered too vague and impalpable.

III

Going from the Grand Canon to Yosemite is going from one sublimity to another of a different order. The canon is the more strange, unearthly, apocryphal, appeals more to the imagination, and is the more overwhelming in its size, its wealth of color, and its multitude of suggestive forms. But for quiet majesty and beauty, with a touch of the sylvan and pastoral, too, Yosemite stands alone. One could live with Yosemite, camp in it, tramp in it, winter and summer in it, and find nature in her tender and human, almost domestic moods, as well as in her grand and austere. But I do not think one could ever feel at home in or near the Grand Canon; it is too unlike anything we have ever known upon the earth; it is like a vision of some strange colossal city uncovered from the depth of geologic time. You may have come to it, as we did, from the Petrified Forests, where you saw the silicified trunks of thousands of gigantic trees or tree ferns, that grew millions of years ago, most of them uncovered, but many of them protruding from banks of clay and gravel, and in their interiors rich in all the colors of the rainbow, and you wonder if you may not now be gazing upon some petrified antediluvian city of temples and holy places exhumed by mysterious hands and opened up to the vulgar gaze of to-day. You look into it from above and from another world and you descend into it at your peril. Yosemite you enter as into a gigantic hall and make your own; the canon you gaze down upon, and are an alien, whether you enter it or not. Yosemite is carved out of the most majestic and enduring of all rocks, granite; the Grand Canon is carved out of one of the most beautiful, but perishable, red Carboniferous sandstone and limestone. There is a maze of beautiful and intricate lines in the latter, a wilderness of temple-like forms and monumental remains, and noble architectural profiles that delight while they bewilder the eye. Yosemite has much greater simplicity, and is much nearer the classic standard of beauty. Its grand and austere features predominate, of course, but underneath these and adorning them are many touches of the idyllic and the picturesque. Its many waterfalls fluttering like white lace against its vertical granite walls, its smooth, level floor, its noble pines and oaks, its open glades, its sheltering groves, its bright, clear, winding river, its soft voice of many waters, its flowers, its birds, its grass, its verdure, even its orchards of blooming apple trees, all inclosed in this tremendous granite frame—what an unforgettable picture it all makes, what a blending of the sublime and the homelike and familiar it all is! It is the waterfalls that make the granite alive, and bursting into bloom as it were. What a touch they give! how they enliven the scene! What music they evoke from these harps of stone!

The first leap of Yosemite Falls is sixteen hundred feet—sixteen hundred feet of a compact mass of snowy rockets shooting downward and bursting into spray around which rainbows flit and hover. The next leap is four hundred feet, and the last six hundred. We tried to get near the foot and inspect the hidden recess in which this airy spirit again took on a more tangible form of still, running water, but the spray over a large area fell like a summer shower, drenching the trees and the rocks, and holding the inquisitive tourist off at a safe distance. We had to beat a retreat with dripping garments before we had got within fifty yards of the foot of the fall. At first I was surprised at the volume of water that came hurrying out of the hidden recess of dripping rocks and trees—a swiftly flowing stream, thirty or forty feet wide, and four or five feet deep. How could that comparatively narrow curtain of white spray up there give birth to such a full robust stream? But I saw that in making the tremendous leap from the top of the precipice, the stream was suddenly drawn out, as we stretch a rubber band in our hands, and that

20

the solid and massive current below was like the rubber again relaxed. The strain was over, and the united waters deepened and slowed up over their rocky bed.

Yosemite for a home or a camp, the Grand Canon for a spectacle. I have spoken of the robin I saw in Yosemite Valley. Think how forlorn and out of place a robin would seem in the Grand Canon! What would he do there? There is no turf for him to inspect, and there are no trees for him to perch on. I should as soon expect to find him amid the pyramids of Egypt, or amid the ruins of Karnak. The bluebird was in the Yosemite also, and the water-ouzel haunted the lucid waters.

I noticed a peculiarity of the oak in Yosemite that I never saw elsewhere [Footnote: I have since observed the same trait in the oaks in Georgia—probably a characteristic of this tree in southern latitudes.]—a fluid or outflowing condition of the growth aboveground, such as one usually sees in the roots of trees—so that it tended to envelop and swallow, as it were, any solid object with which it came in contact. If its trunk touched a point of rock, it would put out great oaken lips several inches in extent as if to draw the rock into its maw. If a dry limb was cut or broken off, a foot from the trunk, these thin oaken lips would slowly creep out and envelop it—a sort of Western omnivorous trait appearing in the trees.

Whitman refers to "the slumbering and liquid trees." These Yosemite oaks recall his expression more surely than any of our Eastern trees.

The reader may create for himself a good image of Yosemite by thinking of a section of seven or eight miles of the Hudson River, midway of its course, as emptied of its water and deepened three thousand feet or more, having the sides nearly vertical, with snow-white waterfalls fluttering against them here and there, the famous spires and domes planted along the rim, and the landscape of groves and glades, with its still, clear winding river, occupying the bottom.

IV

One cannot look upon Yosemite or walk beneath its towering walls without the question arising in his mind, How did all this happen? What were the agents that brought it about? There has been a great geologic drama enacted here; who or what were the star actors? There are two other valleys in this part of the Sierra, Hetch-Hetchy and King's River, that are almost identical in their main features, though the Merced Yosemite is the widest of the three. Each of them is a tremendous chasm in the granite rock, with nearly vertical walls, domes, El Capitans, and Sentinel and Cathedral Rocks, and waterfalls—all modeled on the same general plan. I believe there is nothing just like this trio of Yosemites anywhere else on the globe.

Guided by one's ordinary sense or judgment alone, one's judgment as developed and disciplined by the everyday affairs of life and the everyday course of nature, one would say on beholding Yosemite that here is the work of exceptional and extraordinary agents or world-building forces. It is as surprising and exceptional as would be a cathedral in a village street, or a gigantic sequoia in a grove of our balsam firs. The approach to it up the Merced River does not prepare one for any such astonishing spectacle as awaits one. The rushing, foaming water amid the tumbled confusion of huge granite rocks and the open V-shaped valley, are nothing very remarkable or unusual. Then suddenly you are on the threshold of this hall of the elder gods. Demons and furies might lurk in the valley below, but here is the abode of the serene, beneficent Olympian deities. All is so calm, so hushed, so friendly, yet so towering, so stupendous, so unspeakably beautiful. You are in a mansion carved out of the granite foundations of the earth, with walls two or three thousand feet high, hung here and there with snow-white waterfalls, and supporting the blue sky on domes and pinnacles still higher. Oh, the calmness and majesty of the scene! the evidence of such tremendous activity of some force, some agent, and now so tranquil, so sheltering, so beneficent!

That there should be two or three Yosemites in the Sierra not very far apart, all with the main features singularly alike, is very significant—as if this kind of valley was latent in the granite of that region—some peculiarity of rock structure that lends itself readily to these formations. The Sierra lies beyond the southern limit of the great continental ice-sheet of late Tertiary times, but it nursed and reared many local glaciers, and to the eroding power of these its Yosemites are partly due. But water was at work here long before the ice—eating down into the granite and laying open the mountain for the ice to begin its work. Ice may come, and ice may go, says the river, but I go on forever. Water tends to make a V-shaped valley, ice a U-shaped one, though in the Hawaiian Islands, where water erosion alone has taken place, the prevailing form of the valleys is that of the U-shaped. Yosemite approximates to this shape, and ice has certainly played a part in its formation. But the glacier seems to have stopped at the outlet of the great valley; it did not travel beyond the gigantic hall it had helped to excavate. The valley of the Merced from the mouth of Yosemite downward is an open valley strewn with huge angular granite rocks and shows no signs of glaciation whatever. The reason of this abruptness is quite beyond my ken. It is to me a plausible theory that when the granite that forms the Sierra was lifted or squeezed up by the shrinking of the earth, large fissures and crevasses may have occurred, and that Yosemite and kindred valleys may be

21

the result of the action of water and ice in enlarging these original chasms. Little wonder that the earlier geologists, such as Whitney, were led to attribute the exceptional character of these valleys to exceptional and extraordinary agents—to sudden faulting or dislocation of the earth's crust. But geologists are becoming more and more loath to call in the cataclysmal to explain any feature of the topography of the land. Not to the thunder or the lightning, to earthquake or volcano, to the forces of upheaval or dislocation, but to the still, small voice of the rain and the winds, of the frost and the snow,—the gentle forces now and here active all about us, carving the valleys and reducing the mountains, and changing the courses of rivers,—to these, as Lyell taught us, we are to look in nine cases out of ten, yes, in ninety-nine out of a hundred, to account for the configuration of the continents.

The geologists of our day, while not agreeing as to the amount of work done respectively by ice and water, yet agree that to the latter the larger proportion of the excavation is to be ascribed. At any rate between them both they have turned out one of the most beautiful and stupendous pieces of mountain carving to be found upon the earth.

IV
THROUGH THE EYES OF THE GEOLOGIST

I

How habitually we go about over the surface of the earth, delving it or cultivating it or leveling it, without thinking that it has not always been as we now find it, that the mountains were not always mountains, nor the valleys always valleys, nor the plains always plains, nor the sand always sand, nor the clay always clay. Our experience goes but a little way in such matters. Such a thought takes us from human time to God's time, from the horizon of place and years to the horizon of geologic ages. We go about our little affairs in the world, sowing and reaping and building and journeying, like children playing through the halls of their ancestors, without pausing to ask how these things all came about. We do not reflect upon the age of our fields any more than we do upon the size of the globe under our feet: when we become curious about such matters and look upon the mountains as either old or young, or as the subjects of birth, growth, and decay, then we are unconscious geologists. It is to our interest in such things that geology appeals and it is this interest that it stimulates and guides.

What an astonishing revelation, for instance, that the soil was born of the rocks, and is still born of the rocks; that every particle of it was once locked up in the primitive granite and was unlocked by the slow action of the rain and the dews and the snows; that the rocky ribs of the earth were clothed with this fertile soil out of which we came and to which we return by their own decay; that the pulling-down of the inorganic meant the building-up of the organic; that the death of the crystal meant the birth of the cell, and indirectly of you and me and of all that lives upon the earth.

Had there been no soil, had the rocks not decayed, there had been no you and me. Such considerations have long made me feel a keen interest in geology, and especially of late years have stimulated my desire to try to see the earth as the geologist sees it. I have always had a good opinion of the ground underfoot, out of which we all come, and to which we all return; and the story the geologists tell us about it is calculated to enhance greatly that good opinion.

I think that if I could be persuaded, as my fathers were, that the world was made in six days, by the fiat of a supernatural power, I should soon lose my interest in it. Such an account of it takes it out of the realm of human interest, because it takes it out of the realm of natural causation, and places it in the realm of the arbitrary, and non-natural. But to know that it was not made at all, in the mechanical sense, but that it grew—that it is an evolution as much as the life upon the surface, that it has an almost infinite past, that it has been developing and ripening for millions upon millions of years, a veritable apple upon the great sidereal tree, ameliorating from cycle to cycle, mellowing, coloring, sweetening—why, such a revelation adds immensely to our interest in it.

As with nearly everything else, the wonder of the world grows the more we grasp its history. The wonder of life grows the more we consider the chaos of fire and death out of which it came; the wonder of man grows the more we peer into the abyss of geologic time and of low bestial life out of which he came.

Not a tree, not a shrub, not a flower, not a green thing growing, not an insect of an hour, but has a background of a vast aeon of geologic and astronomic time, out of which the forces that shaped it have emerged, and over which the powers of chaos and darkness have failed to prevail.

The modern geologist affords us one of the best illustrations of the uses of the scientific imagination that we can turn to. The scientific imagination seems to be about the latest phase of the evolution of the human mind. This power of interpretation of concrete facts, this Miltonic flight into time and space, into the heavens above, and into the bowels of the earth beneath, and bodying forth a veritable history, a warring of the powers of light and darkness, with the triumph of the angels of light and life, makes Milton's picture seem hollow and unreal. The creative and poetic imagination has undoubtedly already reached its high-water mark. We shall probably never see the great imaginative works of the past surpassed or even equaled. But in the world of scientific discovery and interpretation, we see the imagination working in new fields and under new conditions, and achieving triumphs that mark a new epoch in the history of the race. Nature, which once terrified man and made a coward of him, now inspires him and fills him with love and enthusiasm.

The geologist is the interpreter of the records of the rocks. From a bit of strata here, and a bit there, he re-creates the earth as it was in successive geologic periods, as Cuvier reconstructed his extinct animals from fragments of their bones; and the same interpretative power of the imagination is called into play in both cases, only the palaeontologist has a much narrower field to work in, and the background of his re-creations must be supplied by the geologist.

Everything connected with the history of the earth is on such a vast scale—such a scale of time, such a scale of power, such a scale of movement—that in trying to measure it by our human standards and experience we are like the proverbial child with his cup on the seashore. Looked at from our point of view, the great geological processes often seem engaged in world-destruction rather than in world-building. Those oft-repeated invasions of the continents by the ocean, which have gone on from Archaean times, and during which vast areas which had been dry land for ages were engulfed, seem like world-wide catastrophes. And no doubt they were such to myriads of plants and animals of those times. But this is the way the continents grew. All the forces of the invading waters were engaged in making more land.

The geologist is bold; he is made so by the facts and processes with which he deals; his daring affirmations are inspired by a study of the features of the earth about him; his time is not our time, his horizons are not our horizons; he escapes from our human experiences and standards into the vast out-of-doors of the geologic forces and geologic ages. The text he deciphers is written large, written across the face of the continent, written in mountain-chains and ocean depths, and in the piled strata of the globe. We untrained observers cannot spell out these texts, because they are written large; our vision is adjusted to smaller print; we are like the school-boy who finds on the map the name of a town or a river, but does not see the name of the state or the continent printed across it. If the geologist did not tell us, how should we ever suspect that probably where we now stand two or more miles of strata have been worn away by the winds and rains; that the soil of our garden, our farm, represents the ashes of mountains burned up in the slow fires of the geologic ages.

Geology first gives us an adequate conception of time. The limitations which shut our fathers into the narrow close of six thousand years are taken down by this great science and we are turned out into the open of unnumbered millions of years. Upon the background of geologic time our chronological time shows no more than a speck upon the sky. The whole of human history is but a mere fraction of a degree of this mighty arc. The Christian era would make but a few seconds of the vast cycle of the earth's history. Geologic time! The words seem to ring down through the rocky strata of the earth's crust; they reverberate under the mountains, and make them rise and fall like the waves of the sea; they open up vistas through which we behold the continents and the oceans changing places, and the climates of the globe shifting like clouds in the sky; whole races and tribes of animal forms disappear and new ones come upon the scene. Such a past! the imagination can barely skirt the edge of it. As the pool in the field is to the sea that wraps the earth, so is the time of our histories to the cycle of ages in which the geologist reckons the events of the earth's history.

Through the eyes of the geologist one may look upon his native hills and see them as they were incalculable ages ago, and as they probably will be incalculable ages ahead; those hills, so unchanging during his lifetime, and during a thousand lifetimes, he may see as flitting as the cloud shadows upon the landscape. Out of the dark abyss of geologic time there come stalking the ghosts of lost mountains and lost hills and valleys and plains, or lost rivers and lakes, yea, of lost continents; we see a procession of the phantoms of strange and monstrous beasts, many of them colossal in size and fearful in form, and among the minor forms of this fearful troop of spectres we see the ones that carried safely forward, through the vicissitudes of those ages, the precious impulse that was to eventuate in the human race.

Only the geologist knows the part played by erosion in shaping the earth's surface as we see it. He sees, I repeat, the phantoms of vanished hills and mountains all about us. He sees their shadow forms wherever he looks. He follows out the lines of the flexed or folded strata where they come to the surface, and thus sketches in the air the elevation that has disappeared. In some places he finds that the valleys have become hills and the hills have become valleys, or that the anticlines and synclines, as he calls them, have changed places—as a result of the unequal hardness of the rocks. Over all the older parts of the country the original features have been so changed by erosion that, could they be suddenly restored, one would be lost on his home farm. The rocks have melted into soil, as the snow-banks in spring melt into water. The rocks that remain are like fragments of snow or ice that have so far withstood the weather. Geologists tell us that the great Appalachian chain has been in the course of the ages reduced almost to a base level or peneplain, and then reelevated and its hills and mountains carved out anew.

We change the surface of the earth a little with our engineering, drain a marsh, level a hill, sweep away a forest, or bore a mountain, but what are these compared with the changes that have gone on there before our race was heard of? In my native mountains, the Catskills, all those peaceful pastoral valleys, with their farms and homesteads, lie two or three thousand feet below the original surface of the land. Could the land be restored again to its first condition in Devonian times, probably the fields where I hoed corn and potatoes as a boy would be buried one or two miles beneath the rocks.

The Catskills are residual mountains, or what Agassiz calls "denudation mountains." When we look at them with the eye of the geologist we see the great plateau of tableland of Devonian times out of which they were carved by the slow action of the sub-aerial forces. They are like the little ridges and mounds of soil that remain of your garden-patch after the waters of a cloudburst have swept over it. They are immeasurably old, but they do not look it, except to the eye of the geologist. There is nothing decrepit in their appearance, nothing broken, or angular, or gaunt, or rawboned. Their long, easy, flowing lines, their broad, smooth backs, their deep, wide, gently sloping valleys, all help to give them a look of repose and serenity, as if the fret and fever of life were long since passed with them. Compared with the newer mountains of uplift in the West, they are like cattle lying down and ruminating in the field beside alert wild steers with rigid limbs and tossing horns. They sleep and dream with bowed heads upon the landscape. Their great flanks and backs are covered with a deep soil that nourishes a very even growth of beech, birch, and maple forests. Though so old, their tranquillity never seems to have been disturbed; no storm-and-stress period has left its mark upon them. Their strata all lie horizontal just as they were laid down in the old seas, and nothing but the slow gentle passage of the hand of time shows in their contours. Mountains of peace and repose, hills and valleys with the flowing lines of youth, coming down to us from the fore- world of Palaeozoic time, yet only rounded and mellowed by the aeons they have passed through. Old, oh, so old, but young with verdure and limpid streams, and the pastoral spirit of to-day!

To the geologist most mountains are short-lived. When he finds great sturdy ranges, like the Alps, the Andes, the Himalayas, he knows they are young,—mere boys. When they get old, they will be cut down, and their pride and glory gone. A few more of these geologic years and they will be reduced to a peneplain,—only their stumps left. This seems to hold truer of mountains that are wrinkles in the earth's crust—squeezed up and crumpled stratified rock, such as most of the great mountain-systems are—than of mountains of erosion like the Catskills, or of upheaval like the Adirondacks. The crushed and folded and dislocated strata are laid open to the weather as the horizontal strata, and as the upheaved masses of Archaean rock are not. Moreover, strata of unequal hardness are exposed, and this condition favors rapid erosion.

In imagination the geologist is present at the birth of whole mountain-ranges. He sees them gestating in the womb of their mother, the sea. Where our great Appalachian range now stands, he sees, in the great interior sea of Palaeozoic time, what he calls a "geosyncline," a vast trough, or cradle, being slowly filled with sediment brought down by the rivers from the adjoining shores. These sediments accumulate to the enormous depth of twenty-five thousand feet, and harden into rock. Then in the course of time they are squeezed together and forced up by the contraction of the earth's crust, and thus the Appalachians are born. When Mother Earth takes a new hitch in her belt, her rocky garment takes on new wrinkles. Just why the earth's crust should wrinkle along lines of rock of such enormous thickness is not a little puzzling. But we are told it is because this heavy mass of sediment presses the sea-bottom down till the rocks are fused by the internal heat of the earth and thus a line of weakness is established. In any case the earth's forces act as a whole, and the earth's crust at the thickest points is so comparatively thin— probably not much more than a heavy sheet of cardboard over a six-inch globe—that these forces seem to go their own way regardless of such minor differences.

The Alps and the Himalayas, much younger than our Appalachians, were also begotten and nursed in the cradle of a vast geosyncline in the Tertiary seas. We speak of the birth of a mountain-range in terms of a common human occurrence, or as if it were an event that might be witnessed, measurable in human years or days, whereas it is an event measurable only in geologic periods, and geologic periods are marked off only on the dial-face of eternity. The old Hebrew writer gave but a faint image of it when he said that with the Lord a thousand years are as one day; it is hardly one hour of the slow beat of that clock whose hours mark the periods of the earth's development.

The whole long period during which the race of man has been rushing about, tickling and scratching and gashing the surface of the globe, would make but a small fraction of one of the days that make up the periods with which the geologist deals. And the span of human life, how it dwindles to a point in the face of the records of the rocks! Doubtless the birth of some of the mountain-systems of the globe is still going on, and we suspect it not; an elevation of one foot in a century would lift up the Sierra or the Rocky Mountains in a comparatively short geologic period.

II

It was the geologist that emboldened Tennyson to sing,—

"The hills are shadows and they flow
From form to form and nothing stands,
They melt like mists, the solid lands,
Like clouds they shape themselves and go."

But some hills flow much faster than others. Hills made up of the latest or newest formations seem to take to themselves wings the fastest.

The Archaean hills and mountains, how slowly they melt away! In the Adirondacks, in northern New England, in the Highlands of the Hudson, they still hold their heads high and have something of the vigor of their prime.

The most enduring rocks are the oldest; and the most perishable are, as a rule, the youngest. It takes time to season and harden the rocks, as it does men. Then the earlier rocks seem to have had better stuff in them. They are nearer the paternal granite; and the primordial seas that mothered them were, no doubt, richer in the various mineral solutions that knitted and compacted the sedimentary deposits. The Cretaceous formations melt away almost like snow. I fancy that the ocean now, compared with the earlier condition when it must have been so saturated with mineral elements, is like thrice-skimmed milk.

The geologist is not stinted for time. He deals with big figures. It is refreshing to see him dealing out his years so liberally. Do you want a million or two to account for this or that? You shall have it for the asking. He has an enormous balance in the bank of Time, and he draws upon it to suit his purpose. In human history a thousand years is a long time. Ten thousand years wipe out human history completely. Ten thousand more, and we are probably among the rude cave-men or river-drift men. One hundred thousand, and we are—where? Probably among the simian ancestors of man. A million years, and we are probably in Eocene or Miocene times, among the huge and often grotesque mammals, and our ancestor, a little creature, probably of the marsupial kind, is skulking about and hiding from the great carnivorous beasts that would devour him.

"Little man, least of all,
Among the legs of his guardians tall,
Walked about with puzzled look.
Him by the hand dear Nature took,
Dearest Nature, strong and kind,
Whispered, 'Darling, never mind!
To-morrow they will wear another face,
The founder thou; these are thy race!'"

I fancy Emerson would be surprised and probably displeased at the use I have made of his lines. I remember once hearing him say that his teacher in such matters as I am here touching upon was Agassiz, and not Darwin. Yet did he not write that audacious line about "the worm striving to be man"? And Nature certainly took his "little man" by the hand and led him forward, and on the morrow the rest of the animal creation "wore another face."

III

In my geological studies I have had a good deal of trouble with the sedimentary rocks, trying to trace their genealogy and getting them properly fathered and mothered. I do not think the geologists fully appreciate what a difficult problem the origin of these rocks presents to the lay mind. They bulk so large, while the mass of original crystalline rocks from which they are supposed to have been derived is so small in comparison. In the case of our own continent we have, to begin with, about two million of square miles of Archaean rocks in detached lines and masses, rising here and there above the primordial ocean; a large triangular mass in Canada, and two broken lines of smaller masses running south from it on each side of the continent, inclosing a vast interior sea between them. To end with, we have the finished continent of eight million or more square miles, of an average height of two thousand feet above the sea, built up or developed from and around these granite centres very much as the body is built up and around the bones, and of such prodigious weight that some of our later geologists seek to account for the continental submarine shelf that surrounds the continent on the theory that the land has slowly crept out into the sea under the pressure of its own weight. And all this, to say nothing of the vast amount of rock, in some places a mile or two in thickness, that has been eroded from the land surfaces of the globe in later geological time, and now lies buried in the seas and lakes,—we are told, is the contribution of those detached portions of Archaean rock that first rose above the primordial seas. It is a greater miracle than that of the loaves and the fishes. We have vastly more to end with than we had to begin with. The more the rocks have been destroyed, the more they have increased; the more the waters have devoured them, the more they have multiplied and waxed strong.

Either the geologists have greatly underestimated the amount of Archaean rock above the waters at the start, or else there are factors in the problem that have not been taken into the account. Lyell seems to have appreciated the difficulties of the problem, and, to account for the forty thousand feet of sediment deposited in Palaeozoic times in the region of the Appalachians, he presupposes a neighboring continent to the east, probably formed of Laurentian rocks, where now rolls the Atlantic. But if such a continent once existed, would not some vestige of it still remain? The fact that no trace of it as been found, it seems to me, invalidates Lyell's theory.

Archaean time in geologic history answers to pre-historic time in human history; all is dark and uncertain, though we are probably safe in assuming that there was more strife and turmoil among the earth-building forces than there has ever been since. The body of unstratified rock within the limits of North America may have been much greater than is supposed, but it seems to me impossible that it could have been anything like as massive as the continent now is. If this had been the case there would have been no great interior sea, and no wide sea-margins in which the sediments of the stratified rocks could have been deposited. More than four fifths of the continent is of secondary origin and shows that vast geologic eras went to the making of it.

It is equally hard to believe that the primary or igneous rocks, where they did appear, were sufficiently elevated to have furnished through erosion the all but incalculable amount of material that went to the making of our vast land areas. But the geologists give me the impression that this is what we are to believe.

Chamberlin and Salisbury, in their recent college geology, teach that each new formation implies the destruction of an equivalent amount of older rock—every system being entirely built up out of the older one beneath it. Lyell and Dana teach the same thing. If this were true, could there have been any continental growth at all? Could a city grow by the process of pulling down the old buildings for material to build the new? If the geology is correct, I fail to see how there would be any more land surface to-day then there was in Archaean times. Each new formation would only have replaced the old from which it came. The Silurian would only have made good the waste of the Cambrian, and the Devonian made good the waste of the Silurian, and so on to the top of the series, and in the end we should still have been at the foot of the stairs. That vast interior sea that in Archaean times stretched from the rudimentary Appalachian Mountains to the rudimentary Rocky Mountains, and which is now the heart of the continent, would still have been a part of the primordial ocean. But instead of that, this sea is filled and piled up with sedimentary rocks thousands of feet thick, that have given birth on their surfaces to thousands of square miles of as fertile soil as the earth holds.

That the original crystalline rocks played the major part in the genealogy of the subsequent stratified rocks, it would be folly to deny. But it seems to me that chemical and cosmic processes, working through the air and the water, have contributed more than they have been credited with.

It looks as if in all cases when the soil is carried to the seabottom as sediment, and again, during the course of ages, consolidated into rocks, the rocks thus formed have exceeded in bulk the rocks that gave them birth. Something analogous to vital growth takes place. It seems as if the original granite centres set the world-building forces at work. They served as nuclei around which the materials gathered. These rocks bred other rocks, and these still others, and yet others, till the framework of the land was fairly established. They were like the pioneer settlers who plant homes here and there in the wilderness, and then in due time all the land is peopled.

The granite is the Adam rock, and through a long line of descent the major part of all the other rocks directly or indirectly may be traced. Thus the granite begot the Algonquin, the Algonquin begot the Cambrian, the Cambrian begot the Silurian, the Silurian begot the Devonian, and so on up through the Carboniferous, the Permian, the Mesozoic rocks, the Tertiary rocks, to the latest Quaternary deposit.

But the curious thing about it all is the enormous progeny from so small a beginning; the rocks seem really to have grown and multiplied like organic beings; the seed of the granite seems to have fertilized the whole world of waters, and in due time they brought forth this huge family of stratified rocks. There stands the Archaean Adam, his head and chest in Canada, his two unequal legs running, one down the Pacific coast, and one down the Atlantic Coast, and from his loins, we are told, all the progeny of rocks and soils that make up the continent have sprung, one generation succeeding another in regular order. His latest offspring is in the South and Southwest, and in the interior. These are the new countries, geologically speaking, as well as humanly speaking.

The great interior sea, epicontinental, the geologists call it, seems to have been fermenting and laboring for untold aeons in building up these parts of the continent. In the older Eastern States we find the sons and grandsons of the old Adam granite; but in the South and West we find his offspring of the twentieth or twenty-fifth generation, and so unlike their forebears; the Permian rocks, for instance, and the Cretaceous rocks, are soft and unenduring, for the most part. The later slates, too, are degenerates, and much of the sandstones have the hearts of prodigals. In the Bad Lands of Arizona I could have cut my way into some of the Eocene formations with my pocket-knife. Apparently the farther away we get from the parent granite, the more easily is the rock eroded. Nearly all the wonderful and beautiful sculpturing of the rocks in the West and Southwest is in rocks of comparatively recent date.

Can we say that all the organic matter of our time is from preexisting organic matter? one organism torn down to build up another? that the beginning of the series was as great as the end? There may have been as much matter in a state of vital organization in Carboniferous or in Cretaceous times as in our own, but there is certainly more now than in early Palaeozoic times. Yet every grain of this matter has existed somewhere in some form for all time. Or we might ask if all the wealth of our day is from preexisting wealth—one fortune pulled down to build up another,—too often the case, it is true,—thus passing the accumulated wealth along from one generation to another. On the contrary, has there not been a steady gain of that we call wealth through the ingenuity and the industry of man directed towards the latent wealth of the earth? In a parallel manner has there been a gain in the bulk of the secondary rocks through the action of the world-building forces directed to the sea, the air, and the preexisting rocks. Had there been no gain, the fact would suggest the ill luck of a man investing his capital in business and turning it over and over, and having no more money at the end than he had in the beginning.

Nothing is in the sedimentary rock that was not at one time in the original granite, or in the primordial seas, or in the primordial atmosphere, or in the heavens above, or in the interior of the earth beneath. We must sweep the heavens, strain the seas, and leach the air, to obtain all this material. Evidently the growth of these rocks has been mainly a chemical process—a chemical organization of preexisting material, as much so as the growth of a plant or a tree or an animal. The color and texture and volume of each formation differ so radically from those of the one immediately before it as to suggest something more than a mere mechanical derivation of one from the other. New factors, new sources, are implied. "The farther we recede from the present time," says Lyell, "and the higher the antiquity of the formations which we examine, the greater are the changes which the sedimentary deposits have undergone." Above all have chemical processes produced changes. This constant passage of the mineral elements of the rocks through the cycle of erosion, sedimentation, and reinduration has exposed them to the action of the air, the light, the sea, and has thus undoubtedly brought about a steady growth in their volume and a constant change in their color and texture. Marl and clay and green sand and salt and gypsum and shale, all have their genesis, all came down to us in some way or in some degree, from the aboriginal crystalline rocks; but what transformations and transmutations they have undergone! They have passed through Nature's laboratory and taken on new forms and characteristics.

"All sediments deposited in the sea," says my geology, "undergo more or less chemical change," and many chemical changes involve notable changes in volume of the mineral matter concerned. It has been estimated that the conversion of granite rock into soil increases its volume eighty-eight per cent, largely as the result of hydration, or the taking up of water in the chemical union. The processes of oxidation and carbonation are also expansive processes. Whether any of this gain in volume is lost in the process of sedimentation and reconsolidation, I do not know. Probably all the elements that water takes from the rocks by solution, it returns to them when the disintegrated parts, in the form of sediment in the sea, is again converted into strata. It is in this cycle of rock disintegration and rock re-formation that the processes of life go on. Without the decay of the rock there could be no life on the land. Water and air are always the go-betweens of the organic and inorganic. After the rains have depleted the rocks of their soluble parts and carried them to the sea, they come back and aid vegetable life to unlock and appropriate other soluble parts, and thus build up the vegetable and, indirectly, the animal world.

That the growth of the continents owes much to the denudation of the sea-bottom, brought about by the tides and the ocean-currents, which were probably much more powerful in early than in late geologic times, and to submarine mineral springs and volcanic eruptions of ashes and mud, admits of little doubt. That it owes much to extra-terrestrial sources—to meteorites and meteoric dust—also admits of little doubt.

27

It seems reasonable that earlier in the history of the evolution of our solar system there should have been much more meteoric matter drifting through the interplanetary spaces than during the later ages, and that a large amount of this matter should have found its way to the earth, in the form either of solids or of gases. Probably much more material has been contributed by volcanic eruptions than there is any evidence of apparent. The amount of mineral matter held in solution by the primordial seas must have been enormous. The amount of rock laid down in Palaeozoic times is estimated at fifty thousand feet, and of this thirteen thousand feet were limestone; while the amount laid down in Mesozoic times, for aught we know a period quite as long, amounts to eight thousand feet, indicating, it seems to me, that the deposition of sediment went on much more rapidly in early geologic times. We are nearer the beginning of things. All chemical processes in the earth's crust were probably more rapid. Doubtless the rainfall was more, but the land areas must have been less. The greater amount of carbon dioxide in the air during Palaeozoic times would have favored more rapid carbonation. When granite is dissolved by weathering, carbon unites with the potash, the soda, the lime, the magnesia, and the iron, and turns them into carbonates and swells their bulk. The one thing that is passed along from formation to formation unchanged is the quartz sand. Quartz is tough, and the sand we find to-day is practically the same that was dissolved out of the first crystalline rocks.

Take out of the soil and out of the rocks all that they owe to the air,—the oxygen and the carbon,—and how would they dwindle! The limestone rocks would practically disappear.

Probably not less that one fourth of all the sedimentary rocks are limestone, which is of animal origin. How much of the lime of which these rocks were built was leached out of the land-areas, and how much was held in solution by the original sea-water, is of course a question. But all the carbon they hold came out of the air. The waters of the primordial ocean were probably highly charged with mineral matter, with various chlorides and sulphates and carbonates, such as the sulphate of soda, the sulphate of lime, the sulphate of magnesia, the chloride of sodium, and the like. The chloride of sodium, or salt, remains, while most of the other compounds have been precipitated through the agency of minute forms of life, and now form parts of the soil and of the stratified rocks beneath it.

If the original granite is the father of the rocks, the sea is the mother. In her womb they were gestated and formed. Had not this seesaw of land and ocean taken place, there could have been no continental growth. Every time the land took a bath in the sea, it came up enriched and augmented. Each new layer of rocky strata taken on showed a marked change in color and texture. It was a kind of evolution from that which preceded it. Whether the land always went down, or whether the sea at times came up, by reason of some disturbance of the ocean floors in its abysmal depths, we have no means of knowing. In any case, most of the land has taken a sea bath many times, not all taking the plunge at the same time, but different parts going down in successive geologic ages. The original granite upheavals in British America, and in New York and New England, seem never to have taken this plunge, except an area about Lake Superior which geologists say has gone down four or five times. The Laurentian and Adirondack ranges have never been in pickle in the sea since they first saw the light. In most other parts of the continent, the seesaw between the sea and the land has gone on steadily from the first, and has been the chief means of the upbuilding of the land.

To the slow and oft-repeated labor-throes of the sea we owe the continents. But the sea devours her children. Large areas, probably continental in extent, have gone down and have not yet come up, if they ever will. The great Mississippi Valley was under water and above water time after time during the Palaeozoic period. The last great invasion of the land by the sea, and probably the greatest of all, seems to have been in Cretaceous times, at the end of the Mesozoic period. There were many minor invasions during Tertiary times, but none on so large a scale as this Cretaceous invasion. At this time a large part of North and South America, and of Europe, and parts of Asia and Australia went under the ocean. It was as if the earth had exhaled her breath and let her abdomen fall. The sea united the Gulf of Mexico with the Arctic Ocean, and covered the Prairie and the Gulf States and came up over New Jersey to the foot of the Archaean Highlands. This great marine inundation probably took place several million years ago. It was this visitation of the sea that added the vast chalk beds to England and France. In parts of this country limestone beds five or six thousand feet thick were laid down, as well as extensive chalk beds. The earth seems to have taken another hitch in her girdle during this era. As the land went down, the mountains came up. Most of the great Western mountain-chains were formed during this movement, and the mountains of Mexico were pushed up. The Alps were still under the sea, but the Sierra and the Alleghanies were again lifted.

It is very interesting to me to know that in Colorado charred wood, and even charcoal, have been found in Cretaceous deposits. The fact seems to give a human touch to that long-gone time. It was, of course, long ages before the evolution of man, as man, had taken place, yet such is the power of

28

association, that those charred sticks instantly call him to mind, as if we had come upon the place of his last campfire. At any rate, it is something to know that man, when he did come, did not have to discover or invent fire, but that this element, which has played such a large part in his development and civilization, was here before him, waiting, like so many other things in nature, to be his servant and friend. As Vulcan was everywhere rampant during this age, throwing out enough lava in India alone to put a lava blanket four or five feet thick over the whole surface of the globe, it was probably this fire that charred the wood. It would be interesting to know if these enormous lava-flows always followed the subsidence of some part of the earth's crust. In Cretaceous times both the subsidence and the lava- flows seem to have been worldwide.

IV

We seem to think that the earth has sown all her wild oats, that her riotous youth is far behind her, and that she is now passing into a serene old age. Had we lived during any of the great periods of the past, we might have had the same impression, so tranquil, for the most part, has been the earth's history, so slow and rhythmical have been the beats of the great clock of time. We see this in the homogeneity of the stratified rocks, layer upon layer for thousands of feet as uniform in texture and quality as the goods a modern factory turns out, every yard of it like every other yard. No hitch or break anywhere. The bedding-planes of many kinds of rock occur at as regular intervals as if they had been determined by some kind of machinery. Here, on the formation where I live, there are alternate layers of slate and sandstone, three or four inches thick, for thousands of feet in extent; they succeed each other as regularly as the bricks and mortar in a brick wall, and are quite as homogeneous. What does this mean but that for an incalculable period the processes of erosion and deposition went on as tranquilly as a summer day? There was no strike among the workmen, and no change in the plan of the building, or in the material.

The Silurian limestone, the old red sandstone, the Hamilton flag, the Oneida conglomerate, where I have known them, are as homogeneous as a snowbank, or as the ice on a mountain lake; grain upon grain, all from the same source in each case, and sifted and sorted by the same agents, and the finished product as uniform in color and quality as the output of some great mill.

Then, after a vast interval, there comes a break: something like an end and a new beginning, as if one day of creation were finished and a new one begun. The different formations lie unconformably upon each other, which means revolution of some sort. There has been a strike or a riot in the great mill, or it has lain idle for a long period, and when it has resumed, a different product is the result. Something happened between each two layers. What?

Though in remote geological ages the earth-building and earth-shaping forces were undoubtedly more active than they are now, and periods of deformation and upheaval were more frequent, yet had we lived in any of those periods we should probably have found the course of nature, certainly when measured by human generations, as even and tranquil as we find it to-day. The great movements are so slow and gentle, for the most part, that we should not have been aware of them had we been on the spot. Once in a million or a half-million years there may have been terrific earthquakes and volcanic eruptions, such as seem to have taken place in Tertiary time, and at the end of the Palaeozoic period. Yet the vast stretches of time between were evidently times of tranquillity.

It is probable that the great glacial winter of Pleistocene times came on as gradually as our own winter, or through a long period of slowly falling temperature, and as it seems to have been many hundred thousand times as long, this preceding period, or great fall, was probably equally long—so long that the whole of recorded human history would form but a small fraction of it. It may easily be, I think, that we are now living in the spring of the great cycle of geologic seasons. The great ice-sheet has withdrawn into the Far North like snowbanks that linger in our wood in late spring, where it still covers Greenland as it once covered this country. When the season of summer is reached, some hundreds of thousands of years hence, it may be that tropical life, both animal and vegetable, will again flourish on the shores of the Arctic Ocean, as it did in Tertiary times. And all this change will come about so quietly and so slowly that nobody will suspect it.

That the crust of the earth is becoming more and more stable seems a natural conclusion, but that all folding and shearing and disruption of the strata are at an end, is a conclusion we cannot reach in the face of the theory that the earth is shrinking as it cools.

The earth cools and contracts with almost infinite slowness, and the great crustal changes that take place go on, for the most part, so quietly and gently that we should not suspect them were we present on the spot, and long generations would not suspect them. Elevations have taken place across the beds of rivers without deflecting the course of the river; the process was so slow that the river sawed down through the rock as fast as it came up. Nearly all the great cosmic and terrestrial changes and revolutions are veiled from us by this immeasurable lapse of time.

29

Any prediction about the permanence of the land as we know it, or as the race has known it, or of our immunity from earthquakes or volcanic eruptions, or of a change of climate, or of any cosmic catastrophe, based on human experience, is vain and worthless. What is or has been in man's time is no criterion as to what will be in God's time. The periods of great upheaval and deformation in the earth's crust appear to be separated by millions of years. Away back in pre-Cambrian times, there appear to have been immense periods during which the peace and repose of the globe were as profound as in our own time. Then at the end of Palaeozoic time—how many millions of years is only conjectural—the truce of aeons was broken, and the dogs of war let loose; it was a period of revolution which resulted in the making of one of our greatest mountain-systems, the Appalachian, and in an unprecedented extinction of species. Later eras have witnessed similar revolutions. Why may they not come again? The shrinking of the cooling globe must still go on, and this shrinking must give rise to surface disturbances and dislocations, maybe in the uplift of new mountain-ranges from the sea-bottom, now undreamed of, and in volcanic eruptions as great as any in the past. Such a shrinkage and eruption made the Hawaiian Islands, probably in Tertiary times; such a shrinkage may make other islands and other continents before another period of equal time has elapsed.

Of course the periods and eras into which the geologists divide geologic time are as arbitrary as the months and seasons into which we divide our year, and they fade out into each other in much the same way; but they are really as marked as our seasonal divisions. Not in their climates—for the climate of the globe seems to have been uniformly warm from pole to pole, without climatic zones, throughout the vast stretch of Palaeozoic and Mesozoic times—but in the succession of animal and vegetable life which they show. The rocks are the cemeteries of the different forms of life that have appeared upon the globe, and here the geologist reads their succession in time, and assigns them to his geologic horizons accordingly. The same or allied forms appeared upon all parts of the earth at approximately the same time, so that he can trace his different formations around the world by the fossils they hold. Each period had its dominant forms. The Silurian was the great age of trilobites; the Devonian, the age of fishes; Mesozoic times swarm with the gigantic reptiles; and in Tertiary times the mammals are dominant. Each period and era has its root in that which preceded it. There were rude, half-defined fishes in the Silurian, and probably the beginning of amphibians in the Devonian, and some small mammalian forms in the Mesozoic time, and doubtless rude studies of the genus Homo in Tertiary times. Nature works up her higher forms like a human inventor from rude beginnings. Her first models barely suggest her later achievements.

In the vegetable world it has been the same; from the first simple algae in the Cambrian seas up to the forests of our own times, the gradation is easily traced. Step by step has vegetable life mounted. The great majority of the plants and animals of one period fail to pass over into the next, just as our spring flowers fail to pass over into summer, and our summer flowers into fall. But the law of evolution is at work, and life always rises on stepping-stones of its dead self to higher things.

V

HOLIDAYS IN HAWAII

I

On the edge of the world my islands lie," sings Mrs. Frear in her little lyric on the Hawaiian Islands.
    "On the edge of the world my islands lie,
Under the sun-steeped sky;
  And their waving palms
  Are bounteous alms
To the soul-spent passer-by.
        "On the edge of the world my islands sleep
In a slumber soft and deep.
  What should they know
  Of a world of woe,
And myriad men that weep?"

On the rim of the world my fancy seemed to see them that May day when we went aboard the huge Pacific steamship in San Francisco Harbor, and she pointed her prow westward toward the vast wilderness of the Pacific—on the edge of the world, looking out and down across the vast water toward Asia and Australia. I wondered if the great iron ship could find them, and if we should realize or visualize the geography or the astronomy when we got there, and see ourselves on the huge rotundity of the globe not far above her equatorial girdle.

Yes, on the rim of the world they lie to the traveler steaming toward them, and on the rim of the world they lie in his memory after his return, basking there in that tropical sunlight, forever fanned by those cooling trade winds, and encompassed by that morning-glory sea. With my mind's eye I behold

30

them rising from that enormous abyss of the Pacific, fire-born and rain-carved, vast volcanic mountains miles deep under the sea, and in some cases miles high above it, clothed with verdure and teeming with life, the scene of long-gone cosmic strife and destruction, now the abode of rural and civic peace and plenty.

The Pacific treated me so much better than the Atlantic ever had that I am probably inclined to overestimate everything I saw on the voyage. It was the first trip at sea that ever gave me any pleasure. The huge vessels are in themselves a great comfort, and in the placid waters and the sliding down the rotund side of the great globe under warmer and warmer skies one gains a very agreeable experience. The first day's run must have carried us out and over that huge Pacific abyss, the Tuscarora Deep, where there were nearly four miles of water under us. Some of our aeroplanes have gone up half that distance and disappeared from sight. I fancy that our ship, more than six hundred feet long, would have appeared a very small object, floating across this briny firmament, could one have looked up at it from the bottom of that sea.

The Hawaiian Islands rise from the border of that vast deep, and one can fancy how that huge pot must have boiled back in Tertiary times, when the red-hot lava of which they are mainly built up was poured from the interior of the globe.

Softer and more balmy grew the air every day, more and more placid and richly tinted grew the sea, till, on the morning of the sixth day, we saw ahead of us, low on the horizon, the dim outlines of the mountains of Molokai. The island of Oahu, upon which Honolulu is situated, was soon in sight. It was not long before we saw Diamond Head, a vast crater bowl, eight hundred feet high on its ocean side, and half a mile across, sitting there upon the shore like some huge, strange work of man's hand, running back through the hills with a level rim, and seaward with a sloping base, brown and ribbed, and in every way unique and striking.

We were approaching a land the child of tropic seas and volcanic lava, and many of the features were new and strange to us. The mountains looked familiar in outline, but the colors of the landscape, the soft lilacs, greens, and browns, and the whole atmosphere of the scene, were unlike anything we had ever before seen. And Diamond Head, what a feature it was! Had it only had a head, one could easily have seen in it a suggestion of a couchant lion, bony, huge, and tawny, looking seaward, and guarding the harbor of Honolulu which lies just behind it. Into this harbor, in the soft morning air, our ship soon found its way, and the monotony of the vast, unpeopled sea was quickly succeeded by human scenes of the most varied and animated character, not the least novel of which were the swarms of half-amphibious native boys who surrounded the vessel as she lay at the wharf, and with brown, upturned faces and beckoning hands tempted the passengers to toss dimes into the water. As the coins struck the surface they would dive with the ease and quickness of seals, and seize the silver apparently before it had gone a yard toward the bottom. Holding the coins up to view between the thumb and finger, they would slip them into their mouths and solicit more.

On shore we were greeted with the music of the Royal Hawaiian Band, and a motley crowd of Hawaiians, Japanese, Chinese, Portuguese, and Americans, bearing colored leis, or wreaths of flowers, which they waved at friends on board, and with which they bedecked them as soon as they came off the gangplank. It was a Babel of tongues in which the strange, vowel-choked language of the Hawaiians was conspicuous.

Honolulu is a beautiful city, clean, bright, well ordered, and well appointed,—electric lights, good streets, electric cars, fine hotels and clubs, excellent fire protection, mountain water, libraries, parks, handsome buildings, attractive homes,—in fact, all that we boast of in our home cities. Embosomed in palms, with mangoes, and other tropical trees, with a profusion of gorgeously colored vines and hedges, with spacious, well-kept grounds about the large and comfortable houses in the residential portion—these features, with the ready hospitality of the people, made our hearts warm towards it at once.

Volcanic heights on all the land side look down upon the city. Mount Tantalus, rising four thousand feet above the sea, is just back of it, with its long slopes of volcanic ash and sand now clothed by forests and fertile fields, and a huge ancient crater called the Punch Bowl, born probably on the selfsame day, the geologists think, as Diamond Head, dominates the city in the immediate foreground. If the Punch Bowl were again to overflow with the fiery liquid, the city would soon go up in smoke. But its bowl-like interior is now covered with grass and trees, and presents a scene of the most peaceful, rural character.

The Orient and the Occident meet in Honolulu. There Asia and America join hands. The main features of the city are decidedly American, but the people seen upon the street and at work indoors and out are more than half Oriental. The native population cuts only a small figure. The real workers— carpenters, masons, field hands, and house servants—are mostly Japanese. Virtually all the work of the

31

immense sugar plantations is done by the little brown men and women, while China supplies some of the merchants in the city and the sailors and stewards on the ocean steamers. What admirable servants the Chinese make, so respectful, so prompt, so silent, so quick to comprehend! The Japanese house servants on the islands also give efficient and gracious service.

I had gone to Honolulu reluctantly, but tarried there joyfully. The fine climate, with its even temperature of about eighty degrees Fahrenheit, and with all that is enervating or oppressive in that degree of heat winnowed out of it by the ceaseless trade winds; the almost unbroken sunshine, perfumed now and then by a sprinkle of sunlit rain from the mountains; the wonderful sea laving the shores on the one hand and the cool, cloud-capped, and rain-drenched heights within easy reach on the other; the green, cozy valleys; the broad sweep of plain; the new, strange nature on every side; the novel and delicious fruits; the pepsin-charged papaya, or tree melon, which tickles the palate while it heals and renews the whole digestive system; the mangoes (oh, the mangoes!); the cordiality of the people; the inviting bungalows; the clean streets; the good service everywhere—all made me feel how mistaken was my reluctance.

Most of the Americans one meets there are descendants of the missionaries who went out from New England and New York early in the last century, and one feels at home with them at once. Many of the residents there have been educated in the States. The Governor, Mr. Frear, is a graduate of Yale; his wife is a graduate of Wellesley. One day a charming Southern woman, president of the College Club, invited us to meet the college women of the city. The gathering took place under the trees upon the lawn of one of the older homesteads. There were forty college women present, many of them teachers, from Vassar, Wellesley, Smith, Bryn Mawr, and Barnard. Among them were two girls who had visited me at my cabin, "Slabsides," while they were at Vassar.

Wide as is the world, the traveler is pretty sure to strike threads of relation with his home country wherever he goes. I made the acquaintance in Honolulu of a man from my own county; another, who showed us great kindness, was from an adjoining county; while one day upon the street I was called by name by a man whom I had known as a boy in the town where I now live.

One Saturday a walking-club, largely made up of men and women teachers, whose native Hawaiian name meant "Walkers in Unfrequented Places," asked us to join them in a walk up Palola Valley to the site of an extinct crater well up in the mountains. These walkers in unfrequented places proved to be real walkers, and gave us all and more than we had bargained for—more mud and wet and slippery trails through clinging vines and rank lantana scrub than was good for our shoes and garments or for the bodies inside them. It was a long pull of many miles, at first up the valley over a fair highway, then into the woods on the mountain-side along a trail that was muddy and slippery from the recent showers, and most of the time was buried out of sight beneath the high, coarse stag-horn fern and a thick growth of lantana that met above it as high as our shoulders. A more discouraging mountain climb I never undertook. The vegetation was all novel, but it had that barbaric rankness of all tropical woods, with nothing of the sylvan sweetness and simplicity of our home woods. There were no fine, towering trees, but low, gnarled, and tortuous ones, which, with their hanging vines, like the broken ropes of a ship's rigging, and their parasitic growths, presented a riotous, disheveled appearance.

Nature in the tropics, left to herself, is harsh, aggressive, savage; looks as though she wanted to hang you with her dangling ropes, or impale you on her thorns, or engulf you in her ranks of gigantic ferns. Her mood is never as placid and sane as in the North. There is a tree in the Hawaiian woods that suggests a tree gone mad. It is called the hau-tree. It lies down, squirms, and wriggles all over the ground like a wounded snake; it gets up, and then takes to earth again. Now it wants to be a vine, now it wants to be a tree. It throws somersaults, it makes itself into loops and rings, it rolls, it reaches, it doubles upon itself. Altogether it is the craziest vegetable growth I ever saw. Where you can get it up off the ground and let it perform its antics on a broad skeleton framework, it makes a cover that no sunbeam can penetrate, and forms a living roof to the most charming verandas—or lanais, as they are called in the islands—that one can wish to see.

But I saw and heard one thing on this walk that struck a different note: it was one of the native birds, the Oahu thrush. The moment I heard it I was reminded of our brown thrasher, though the song, or whistle, was much finer and richer in tone than that of our bird. The glimpse I got of the bird showed it to be of about the size and shape of our thrasher, but much brighter in color. It seems as though the two species must have had a common origin some time, somewhere. I was attracted by no other native bird on this walk. In the valley below we had seen and heard the Chinese workmen going about their rice-fields making strange sounds to drive away the rice-birds, a small, brown species that has been introduced from India.

When we reached the mountain-top, we found it enveloped in fog and mist, and the scene was cold and cheerless. We looked down through a screen of foliage into a deep valley that seemed almost beneath us, and which is supposed to have been an ancient crater. There, on the brink, the walkers had a rude cabin, where we ate our lunch beside a fire and tried to dry our bedraggled garments.

From this point some of the party continued their walk, looking for more unfrequented places, but some of us had longings the other way, and retraced our steps toward the sunlight and the drier winds we had left. We reached town footsore and bedraggled, and the little Japanese who cleaned and pressed my suit of clothes, and made them look as good as new for seventy-five cents, well earned his money.

The walk of eight or ten miles which we took two weeks later with Governor Frear and his wife, up the new Castle trail to the mountain-top behind Tantalus, had some features in common with the first walk,—the increasing mist and coolness as we entered the mountains, the dripping bushes, and the slippery paths,—but we got finer views, and found a better-kept trail. Our walk ended on the top of a narrow ridge of the mountain, where we ate our lunch in a cold, driving mist and were a bit uncomfortable. I was interested in the character of the ridge upon which we sat. It was not more than six feet wide, a screen of volcanic rock worn almost to an edge, and separated two valleys six or seven hundred feet deep. The Governor said he could take me where the dividing ridge between the two valleys was so narrow that one could literally sit astride of it, so that one leg would point to one valley and the other to the other. This is a feature of a new country geologically; the rains and other agents of erosion have whittled the mountains to sharp edges, but have not yet rounded or leveled them.

The northeast trade winds which blow upon these islands nine months in the year bring a burden of moisture from the Pacific which is condensed into rain and mist by the mountains, and which, with the rank vegetation that it fosters, carves them and sharpens them like a great grindstone revolving against their sides. At a place called the Pali—and at the Needles, on the island of Maui—it has worn through the mountain-chain and made deep and very picturesque gorges where, in the case of the Pali, the wind is so strong and steady that you can almost lie down upon it.

It was near the Pali that I saw what I had never seen or heard of before—a waterfall reversed, going up instead of down. It suggested Stockton's story of negative gravity. A small brook comes down off the mountain and attempts to make the leap down a high precipice; but the winds catch it and carry it straight up in the air like smoke. It is translated; it becomes a mere wraith hovering above the beetling crag. Night and day this goes on, the wind snatching from the mountains in this summary way the water it has brought them.

On the walk with the Governor we made the acquaintance of some of the land shells for which these islands are famous—pretty, pearl-like little whorls living on the largest trees, and about the size of a chipping sparrow's egg, with pointed ends, variously colored. There are more than two hundred species on the different islands, I think, each valley having varieties peculiar to itself, showing what a factor isolation is in the evolution of new species. The Governor and his wife, and a young man who had specialized in conchology, plucked them from nearly every bush and tree; but my eye, being untrained in this kind of work, was very slow in finding them.

Coming down from these Hawaiian mountains is like coming out of a dripping tent of clouds into the clear, warm sunshine. The change is most delightful. Your clothing dries very quickly, and chilliness gives place to genial warmth. And the prospects that open before you, the glimpses down into these deep, yellow-green, crater-like valleys, checkered with neat little Chinese farms, the panorama of the city and the sea unrolling as you come down, and always Diamond Head standing guard there to the east—how the vision of it all lingers in the memory!

In climbing the heights, it was always a surprise to me to see the Pacific rise up as I rose, till it stood up like a great blue wall there against the horizon. A level plain unrolls in the same way as we mount above it, but it does not produce the same illusion of rising up like a wall or a mountain-range; the blue, facile water cheats the eye.

One of the novel pleasures in which most travelers indulge while in Honolulu is surf-riding at Waikiki, near Diamond Head. The sea, with a floor of lava and coral, is here shallow for a long distance out, and the surf comes in at intervals like a line of steeds cantering over a plain. We went out in our bathing-suits in a long, heavy dugout, with a lusty native oarsman in each end. When several hundred yards from shore, we saw, on looking seaward, the long, shining billows coming, whereupon our oarsmen headed the canoe toward shore, and plied their paddles with utmost vigor, uttering simultaneously a curious, excited cry. In a moment the breaker caught us and, in some way holding us on its crest, shot us toward the shore like an arrow. The sensation is novel and thrilling. The foam flies; the waters leap about you. You are coasting on the sea, and you shout with delight and pray for the sensation to continue. But it is quickly over. The hurrying breaker slips from under you, and leaves you in the trough, while it goes foaming on the shore. Then you turn about and row out from the shore again, and wait for another chance to be shot toward the land on the foaming crest of a great Pacific wave.

I suppose the trick is in the skill of the oarsmen in holding the boat on the pitch of the billow so that in its rush it takes you with it. The native boys do the feat standing on a plank. I was tempted to try this myself, but of course made a comical failure.

One of my pleasant surprises in Honolulu—one that gave the touch of nature which made me feel less a stranger there—was learning that the European skylark had been introduced and was thriving on the grassy slopes back of the city. The mina, a species of starling from India as large as our robin and rather showily dressed, with a loud, strident voice, I had seen and heard everywhere both in town and country, but he was a stranger and did not appeal to me. But the thought of the skylark brought Shelley and Wordsworth, and English downs and meadows, near to me at once, and I was eager to hear it. So early one morning we left the Pleasanton, our tarrying-place, and climbed the long, pastoral slope above the city, where cattle and horses were grazing, and listened for this minstrel from the motherland. We had not long to wait. Sure enough, not far from us there sprang from the turf Shelley's bird, and went climbing his invisible spiral toward the sky, pouring out those hurried, ecstatic notes, just as I had heard him above the South Downs of England. It was a moment of keen delight to me. The bird soared and hovered, drifting about, as it were, before the impetuous current of his song, with all the joy and abandon with which the poets have credited him. It was like a bit of English literature vocal in the air there above these alien scenes. Presently another went up, and then another, and still another, the singers behaving in every respect as they do by the Avon and the Tweed, and for a moment I seemed to be breathing the air that Wordsworth and Shelley breathed.

If our excursion had taken us only to the island of Oahu and its beautiful city, it would have been eminently worth while, but the last week in May we took what is called the inter-island trip, a six days' voyage among the various islands, when we visited the great extinct crater of Haleakala on Maui, and the active volcano Kilauea on Hawaii. It is a voyage over several rough channels in a small steamer, and my friends said, "If you have not yet paid tribute to Neptune, you will pay it now." But I did not. My companions were prostrated, but I see Neptune respects age, and my slumbers were undisturbed. A wireless message had gone to Mr. Aiken, on the island of Maui, to meet us with his automobile in the morning at the landing at Kahului. We were taken to the shore on a lighter, along with the horses and cargo, and there found our new friend awaiting us.

The great mountain of Haleakala rose up in a long line against the sky on the left, and the deeply eroded and canyoned mountains of the older, or west, end of the island on our right. Toward the latter our guide took us. It was a pleasant spin along the good roads, in the fresh morning air, near the beach, to Wailuku, the shire town of the island, two or three miles distant. Here we were most hospitably entertained in the home of Mr. Penhallow, the director of a large sugar plantation.

Here for the first time in my life I saw a gang of steam plows working, pulled by a stationary engine at each end of the field, and turning over the red, heavy volcanic soil. The work was mainly in the hands of Japanese, and was well done. We afterward saw Japanese by the score, both men and women, planting a large area of newly plowed land with sugar-cane.

After we were rested and refreshed, and had sampled the mangoes that had fallen from a tree near the house, Mr. Aiken took us in his automobile up into the famous Iao Valley, at the mouth of which Wailuku is situated. It is a deep, striking chasm carved out of the mountain by the stream, rank with verdure of various kinds, and looked down upon by sharp peaks and ridges five or six thousand feet high. We soon reached the clear rapid, brawling stream, as bright as a Catskill mountain trout brook, and after a mile or two along its course we came to the end of the road, where we left the machine and took a trail that wound onward and upward over a slippery surface and through dripping bushes, for we here began to reach the skirts of the little showers that almost constantly career over and about the interior of these mountains. I neither saw nor heard a bird or other live thing. Guava apples lay on the ground all along the trail, and one could eat them and not make faces. Some of the sharp, knife-blade ridges that cut down toward us from the higher peaks were very startling, and so steep and high that they could be successfully scaled only by the aid of ropes and ladders. A more striking object-lesson in erosion by rain would be hard to find. There were no naked rocks; short, thick vegetation covered even the steepest slopes, and the vegetable acids which this generated, and the perpetual rains, weathered the mountains down. It soon became so wet that we stopped far short of the head of the valley, and turned back. I wished to look into the great, deep, green amphitheatre which seems to lie at the head, but had glimpses of it only from a distance. How many millenniums will it be, I said to myself, before erosion will have completed its work here, and these thin, high mountain-walls will be in ruins? Surely not many.

34

We returned to the hospitable home we had left, and passed the midday there. In the afternoon Mr. Aiken, guiding our eyes by the forms of trees that cut the horizon-line on the huge flank of Haleakala, pointed out the place of his own homestead, twenty or more miles away. From this point the great mountain appeared like a vast landscape tilted up at an easy angle against the horizon. One could hardly believe it was ten thousand feet high. The machine climbed easily more than half the distance to Mr. Aiken's plantation, which we reached in good time in the afternoon, and where we passed a very enjoyable night. It was a surprise to find swarms of mosquitoes at this altitude, so free from all mosquito-breeding waters. But the house was well protected against them. Mosquitoes, as well as flies and vermin, are not native to the island. They came in ships not very long ago, and are now very troublesome in certain parts. They came round the Horn. Mr. Aiken's house itself came round the Horn seventy or eighty years ago. It is a quaint, New England type of house, and has a very homelike look. In front of it, near the gate, stands a Japanese pine which is an object of veneration to all Japanese who chance to come that way. Often their eyes fill with tears on beholding it, so responsive are the little yellow men to associations of home.

In the morning Mr. Aiken drove us in a wagon to a place he has called "Idlewild," six miles farther up the great slope of the mountain. This slope of Haleakala is like a whole township, diversified with farms and woods, valleys and hills, resting on its elbows, so to speak, and looking out over the Pacific. We could look up to the cloud-line, about seven thousand feet above the sea, and occasionally get a glimpse of the long line of the summit through rifts in the clouds. At Idlewild our expedition, consisting of six mules and four people, was fitted out, and in the early afternoon we started on the trail up the mountain.

For several miles our way led over grassy slopes where cattle were grazing, and above which skylarks were singing. This was one of the happy surprises of the trip—the soaring and singing skylarks. All the way till we reached the cloud-belt, we had the larks pouring down their music from the sky above us. They seemed specially jubilant. It was May in England, too, and they sang as though the spirit of those downs and fells was stirring in their hearts, under alien skies, but true to the memories of home.

Before we reached the summit we came upon another introduction from overseas—the English pheasant. One started up from some bushes only a few yards from the trail, went booming away, and disappeared in a deep gully. A little later another sprang up, uttering a cackling cry as it flew away. We saw three altogether. The only home thing we saw was white clover in patches here and there, and it gave a most welcome touch to the unfamiliar scenes.

The cattle we passed on the way were suffering dreadfully from another introduction from the States—the Texas horn-fly, which had recently made its appearance. The poor beasts were driven half-crazy by it, as their sunken eyes and poor condition plainly showed.

The trail became rougher and steeper as we ascended, and the grass and trees gave place to low, scrubby bushes. We were half an hour or more in the cloud-belt, where the singing skylarks did not follow us. The clouds proved to be as loose of texture and as innocent as any summer fog that loiters in our valleys; but it was good to emerge into the sunshine again, and see the jagged line of the top sensibly nearer, and the canopy of clouds unroll itself beneath us. Far ahead of us and near the summit we saw a band of wild goats—twenty-two, I counted—leisurely grazing along, and now and then casting glances down upon us. They were domestic animals gone wild, and still retained their bizarre colors of white and black. One big black leader with a long beard looked down at us and shook his head threateningly. We reached the summit before the sun reached the horizon, and our eyes looked forth upon a strange world, indeed. On one hand the vast sea of cloud, into which the sun was about to drop, rolled away from the mountain below us, with its white surface and the irregular masses rising up from it, suggesting a sea of floating ice. Through rifts in it we caught occasional glimpses of the Pacific—blue, vague, mystical gulfs that seemed filled with something less substantial than water. On the other hand was the vast crater of Haleakala, two thousand feet deep, and many miles across, in which the shadows were deepening, and which looked like some burned-out Hades.

We stood or sat on the jagged edge and saw the day depart and the night come down, the glory of cloud and sea and sunset on the one hand, and on the other side the fearful chasm of the extinct volcano, red and black and barren, with the hosts of darkness gathering in it. It was like a seat between heaven and hell. Then later, when the Southern Cross came out and rose above the awful gulf, the scene was most impressive.

The crater of Haleakala is said to be the largest extinct crater in the world. To follow all its outlines would lead one a distance of more than twenty miles, but it is so irregular in shape that one gets only a poor conception of its extent in a view from its brink. At its widest part it cannot be more than four or five miles across. It was evidently formed by the whole top of the mountain having been blown out or else sunk down in recent geologic times. The fragments of jagged rock that thickly strew the surface all about the summit look as if they might have fallen there. The floor of the interior of the crater is thickly studded with many minor craters, through which the internal fires found vent after the crater as a whole had ceased to act. They are of the shape of huge haystacks, with a hole in the top, and looked soft and yielding in outline, and in color as though they were composed of soot and brick-dust. One of them is much larger than any of the rest. I thought it might be two hundred feet high. "It is eight hundred," said our guide; yet its summit was more than a thousand feet below the rim upon which we sat.

There has been no eruption in Haleakala since early in the last century. Over a large area of the interior the black lava, cracked and crumpled, meets the eye. Miles down one of its great arms toward the sea, we could see the green lines of vegetation, mostly rank ferns, advancing like an invading army. Far ahead were the skirmishers, loose bands of ferns, with individual plants here and there pushing on over the black, uneven surface toward the secondary craters of the centre. Vegetation was also climbing down the ragged sides of the crater, dropping from rock to rock like an invading host. The ferns, those pioneers of the vegetable world, appear to come first. Their giant progenitors subdued the rocks and made the soil in Carboniferous times, and prepared the way for higher vegetable forms, and now these striplings take up the same task in this primitive world of the crater of Haleakala. Their task is a long and arduous one, much more so than in those parts of the island where the rainfall is more copious; but give them time enough, and the barren lava will all be clothed with verdure. When decomposed and ripened by time, it makes a red, heavy soil that supports many kinds of plants and trees.

The ferns come slowly marching in from without, but in the centre of the crater, on the slopes of the red cones and at their bases, is another plant that seems indigenous, born of the ash and the scoria of the volcano, and that apparently has no chlorophyl in its make-up. This is a striking plant, called the silver sword, from the shape and color of its long, narrow leaves. They are the color of frosted silver, and are curved like a sword. It is a strange apparition, white and delicate and rare, springing up in the crater of a slumbering volcano. A more striking contrast with the atmosphere of the surroundings would be hard to find—a suggestion of peace and purity above the graves of world-destroying forces, an angel of light nourished by the ashes of the demons of death and darkness.

It is claimed by the people of the island that this plant is found in no other place on the globe, but this can hardly be possible. If its evolution took place in one crater, it would take place in another. It consists of a great mass of silvery-white, bristling leaves resting upon the ground, from which rises a stalk, strung with flowers, to the height of five or six feet. It is evidently of the Yucca type of plant, and has met with a singular transformation in the sleeping volcano's mouth, all its harsh and savage character turned into gentleness and grace, its armament of needles and daggers giving place to a soft, silvery down. We did not see the plant growing except at a great distance, through field-glasses, but we saw a photograph of it and a dried specimen after we came down from the summit.

It is an all day's trip down into the crater and back, climbing over sliding sands and loose scoria, and our time was too limited to undertake it. We passed the night on the summit in a rude stone hut, which had a fireplace where the guide made coffee, but we had only the volcanic rock for floor. Upon this we spread our ample supply of blankets, and got such sleep as is to be had on high, cold mountain-tops, where the ribs of the mountain prove to be so much harder than one's own ribs—not a first-class quality of sleep, but better than none.

I arose about two o'clock, and made my way out into the star-blazing night. Such glory of the heavens I had never before seen. I had never before been lifted up so near them, and hence had never before seen them through so rarefied an atmosphere. The clouds and vapors had disappeared, and all the hosts of heaven were magnified. The Milky Way seemed newly paved and swept. There was no wind and no sound. The mighty crater was a gulf of blackness, but the sky blazed with light.

The dawn comes early on such a mountain-top, and before four o'clock we were out under the fading stars. As we had seen the day pass into night, surrounded by these wonderful scenes, now we saw the night pass into day, and the elemental grandeur on every hand reborn before us. There was not a wisp of cloud or fog below us or about us to blur the great picture. The sun came up from behind the vast, long, high wall of the Pacific that filled the eastern horizon, and the shadows fled from the huge pile of mountain in the west. We hung about the rim of the great crater or sat upon the jagged rocks, wrapped in our blankets, till the sun was an hour high.

We got another glimpse of the band of goats picking their way from ledge to ledge far below us on the side of the crater. I saw and heard two or three mina birds fly past, apparently seeking new territory to occupy. These birds are more enterprising than the English sparrows, which also swarm in the island towns but do not brave the mountain-heights. The bird from India seems at home everywhere.

After breakfast we still haunted for an hour or more the brink of the great abyss, where one seemed to feel the pulse of primal time, loath to tear ourselves away, loath also to take a last view of the

36

panorama of land and sea, lit by the morning sun, which spread out far below us. To the southeast we could dimly see the outlines of the island of Hawaii, with a faint gleam of snow on its great mountain Mauna Loa, nearly fourteen thousand feet high. In the northwest a dim, dark mass low in the horizon marked the place of Oahu. The ocean rose in the vast horizon and blended with the sky. The eye could not tell where one ended and the other began.

The mules had had a comfortable night in a rude stone stable against the rocks, and were more eager to hit the down trail than were we. The descent proved more fatiguing than the ascent, the constant plunging motion of the animals' shoulders being a sore trial. We dropped down through the belt of clouds that had begun to form, and out into the grassy region of the singing skylarks, past herds of grazing cattle, and at noon were again at Idlewild, resting our weary limbs and comforting the inner man.

In the afternoon Mr. Aiken drove us back to his home farm, where we again passed a very pleasant night. In the morning I walked with him through his pineapple plantation. It was a new kind of farming and fruit-growing to me. I forget now how many hundred thousand plants his field contained. They are set and cultivated much as cabbage is with us, but present a strangely stiff and forbidding aspect. The first cutting is when the plants are about eighteen months old, one large solid apple from each plant. The second crop is called the "raggoon" crop, and yields two apples from each plant, but smaller and less valuable than the first. The field is then reset. I also walked with Mr. Aiken over some new land he was getting ready for pineapples. It had been densely covered with lantana scrub, and clearing it and grubbing it out had been an heroic task. The lantana takes complete possession of the soil, grows about four or five feet high, and makes a network of roots in the soil that defies anything but a steam plow. The soil is a red, heavy clay, and it made the farmer in me sweat to think of the expenditure of labor necessary to turn a lantana bush into a pineapple field. The redness of this volcanic soil is said to be owing to the fact that the growth of vegetation brings the iron into new combinations with organic acids.

Later in the day we visited the large Baldwin pineapple-canning plant, and were shown the whole process of preparing and canning the fruit, and all but surfeited with the most melting and delicious pineapples it was ever my good luck to taste. The Hawaiian pineapple probably surpasses all others in tenderness and lusciousness, and it loses scarcely any of these qualities in the cans. Ripened in the field, where it grew on the flanks of great Haleakala, and eaten out of hand, it is a dream of tropic lusciousness. The canning is done by an elaborate system of machinery managed by Japanese men and women, the naked hand never coming in contact with the peeled fruit, but protected from it by long, thin rubber gloves. There ought to be a great future for this industry, when Eastern consumers really find out the superior quality of the Hawaiian product.

From Mr. Aiken's house one has a view of the great wall of mountains that form the western and older—older geologically—end of the island, in which lies the famous Iao Valley, which I have already described. We judge, from the much deeper marks of rain erosion, that this end of the island is vastly older than the butt end upon which Haleakala is situated. Haleakala is eroded comparatively little. On all its huge northern slope there is only one considerable gash or gully, and this is probably not many thousand years old; but the northwestern end of the island is worn and carved in the most striking manner. Looking at it that morning, I compared it to my extended, relaxed hand, the northern end being gashed and grooved like the sunken spaces between the fingers, while the southwest end, not more than ten miles distant, was only slightly grooved and more like the solid wrist and back hand. All the rains brought by the northeast trades fall upon the northeast end of the islands. The mountain-peaks on the end hold the clouds and strip them dry, so that little or no rain falls upon the south and southwest sides. This is true of all the islands. One end of each is arid and barren, while the other is wet and verdant. One of the smaller islands, Kahoolawe, I believe, dominated by Maui on the northeast, is said to be drying up and blowing away by inches.

What a spell the mountains do lay upon the clouds everywhere,—the robber mountains,—in these islands exacting the last drop of water of all the ocean-born vapors that pass over them! On the northeast side of the Lahaina district there are valleys four or five thousand feet deep; on the southwest side there are no valleys worth mentioning. The difference in this respect was forcibly brought home to me when, later in the day, we made an automobile trip from Wailuku to Lahaina on the southwest side; in going less than twenty miles we quickly passed from the region of verdant valleys and mountain-slopes into a hard, raw, barren, unweathered region, where there was no soil, and where the rocks looked as crude and forbidding as they must have looked the day they flowed out from the depths as molten lava. In outline the island of Maui suggests a truncated statue, the west end representing the head, very old and wrinkled and grooved by time and trouble, the peninsula the well-proportioned neck, and broad-breasted Haleakala forming the trunk. What a torso it is, fire-born and basking there in the tropic seas!

The oldest island of the Hawaiian group is Kauai, called the garden island, because it has much the deepest and most fertile soil. It shows much more evidence of erosion than any of the other islands. The next in point of erosion, and hence in point of age, is Oahu, upon which Honolulu is situated. Then come Molokai and Maui, the two ends of the latter being of vastly unequal age. Hawaii, the largest of them all, nearly as large as Connecticut, is the youngest of the group, and shows the least effects of erosion. When it is as old as Kauai is now, its two huge mountains, Mauna Loa and Mauna Kea, will probably be cut up into deep valleys and cañons and sharp, high ridges, as are the mountains of Kauai and Oahu. The lapse of time required to bring about such a result is beyond all human calculation. Whether one million or two millions of years would do it, who knows? Those warm tropical rains, aided by the rank vegetation which they beget and support, dissolve the volcanic rock slowly but inevitably.

Through the courtesy of Mr. Lowell, the superintendent, we had that day the pleasure of going through a large sugar-making plant at Paia—one that turns out nearly fifty thousand tons of sugar a year. We saw the cane come in from the fields in one end of the plant, and the dry, warm product being put up in bags at the other. All the latest devices and machinery for sugar-making we saw here in full operation, affording a contrast to the crude and wasteful methods I had seen in the island of Jamaica a few years before.

In the afternoon we availed ourselves of the five or six miles of narrow-gauge railway, the only one on the island, to go from Paia to Wailuku, where we were met by another automobile, which hurried us to Lahaina, where we were to meet the steamer that was to convey us to Hilo, on Hawaii. I say "hurried," but before the journey of twenty-odd miles was half over, we realized the truth of the old adage, "The more haste, the less speed." The automobile began to sulk and finally could be persuaded to go only on the low gear, and to rattle along at about the speed of a man with a horse and buggy. We reached Lahaina just as the boat was entering the harbor.

The next morning we found ourselves steaming along past the high, verdant shores of Hawaii. For fifty miles or more the land presented one unbroken expanse of sugar-cane, suggesting fields of some gigantic yellow-green grass. At Hilo the sun was shining between brief showers, and the air was warm and muggy. It is said to rain there every day in the year, and the lush vegetation made the statement seem credible. Judge Andrews met us at the steamer, and took us to his home for rest and dinner, and was extremely kind to us.

In the mid-afternoon we took the train for Glenwood, thirty miles on our way to the volcano of Kilauea. A large part of the way the road leads through sugar plantations, newly carved out of the koa and tree-fern wilderness that originally covered the volcanic soil. Clusters of the little houses of the Japanese laborers, perched high above the ground on slender posts, were passed here and there. Everywhere we saw wooden aqueducts, or flumes, winding around the contours of the hills and across the little valleys, often on high trestle-work, and partly filled with clear, swift-running water, in which the sugar-cane was transported to the mills.

At Glenwood stages meet the tourists and convey them over a fairly good road that winds through the tree-fern forests to the Volcano House, ten miles away. The beauty of that fern-lined forest, the long, stately plumes of the gigantic ferns meeting the eye everywhere, I shall not soon forget. I saw what appeared to be a large, showy red raspberry growing by the roadside, but I did not find it at all tempting to the taste.

It was dark when we reached the Volcano House, and we saw off to the left a red glow upon the fog-clouds, like the reflected light from a burning barn or house in the country, and inferred at once that it came from the volcano, which it did. From my window that night, as I lay in bed, I could see this same angry glow upon the clouds. The smell of sulphur was in the air about the hotel, and very hot steam was issuing from cracks in the rocks. A party of tourists on horseback, in the spirit of true American hurry, visited the volcano that night, but we chose to wait until the morrow.

The next morning the great crater of Kilauea was filled with fog, but it lifted, and the sun shone before noon. We passed a pleasant forenoon strolling along the tree-fringed brink, looking down eight or nine hundred feet upon its black lava floor, and plucking ohelo berries, which grew there abundantly, a kind of large, red huckleberry that one could eat out of hand, but that one could not get excited over. They were better in a pie than in the hand. Their name seemed to go well with the suggestion of the scenes amid which they grew. Kilauea is a round extinct crater about three miles across and seven or eight hundred feet deep. It has been the scene of terrific explosions in past ages, but it has now dwindled to the small active crater of Halemaumau, which is sunk near the middle of it like a huge pot, two hundred or more feet deep and a thousand feet across.

In the mid-afternoon a party of eight or ten of us on horseback set out to visit the volcano. The trail led down the broken and shelving side of the crater, amid trees and bushes, till it struck the floor of lava at the bottom. In going down I was aware all the time of a beautiful bird-song off on my left, a song almost as sweet as that of our hermit thrush, but of an entirely different order. I think it was the song of one of the honey-suckers, a red bird with black wings that in flight looked like our scarlet tanager.

Our course took us out over the cracked and contorted lava-beds, where no green thing was growing. The forms of the lava-flow suggested mailed and writhing dragons, with horrid, gaping mouths and vicious claws. The lava crunched beneath the horses' feet like shelly and brittle ice. At one point we passed over a wide, jagged crack on a bridge. As we neared the crater, the rocks grew warm, and sulphur and other fumes streaked the air.

When a half-mile from the crater we dismounted, and, leaving our horses in charge of the guide, proceeded on foot over the cracked and heated lava rocks toward the brink of this veritable devil's caldron. The sulphur fumes are so suffocating that it can be approached only on the windward side. The first glance into that fearful pit is all that your imagination can picture it. You look upon the traditional lake of brimstone and fire, and if devils were to appear skipping about over the surface with pitchforks, turning their victims as the cook turns her frying crullers in the sputtering fat, it would not much astonish you. This liquid is rather thick and viscid, but it is boiling furiously. Great masses of it are thrown up forty or fifty feet, and fall with a crash like that of the surf upon the shore. Livid jets are thrown up many feet high against the sides and drip back, cooling quickly as the lava descends. We sat or stood upon the brink, at times almost letting our feet hang over the sides, and shielding our faces from the intense heat with paper masks and veils. It is probably the only place in the world where you can come face to face with the heart of an active volcano. There are no veils of vapor to hide it from you. It appears easy enough to cast a stone into the midst of it, but none of us could quite do it.

The mass of boiling lava is said to be about one and one half acres in extent. Its surface is covered with large masses of floating crust, black and smooth, like leather or roofing-paper, and between these masses, or islands, the molten lava shows in broad, vivid lines. It is never quiet. When not actually boiling, there is a slow circulatory movement, and the great flakes of black crust, suggesting scum, drift across from one end to the other and are drawn under the rocks. At one moment only this movement is apparent, then suddenly the mass begins to boil furiously all over the surface, and you hear dimly the sound of the bursting bubbles and the crash of the falling lava. When this takes place, the black floating masses are broken up and scattered as they are in boiling maple-syrup, but they quickly reunite, and are carried on by the current as before.

Looking upon this scene with the thought of the traditional lake of fire and brimstone of our forefathers in mind, you would say that these black, filthy-looking masses floating about on the surface were the accumulation of all the bad stuff that had been fried out of the poor sinners since hell was invented. How much wickedness and uncharity and evil thought it would represent! If the poor victims were clarified and made purer by the process, then it would seem worth while.

At the Volcano House they keep a book in which tourists write down their impressions of the volcano. A distinguished statesman had been there a few days before us, and had written a long account of his impressions, closing with this oratorical sentence: "No pen, however gifted, can describe, no brush, however brilliant, can portray, the wonders we have been permitted to behold." I could not refrain from writing under it, "I have seen the orthodox hell, and it's the real thing."

That huge kettle of molten metal, mantling and bubbling, how it is impressed upon my memory! It is a vestige of the ancient cosmic fire that once wrapped the whole globe in its embrace. It had a kind of brutal fascination. One could not take one's eyes from it. That network of broad, jagged, fiery lines defining those black, smooth masses, or islands, of floating matter told of a side of nature we had never before seen. We lingered there on the brink of the fearful spectacle till night came on, and the sides of the mighty caldron, and the fog-clouds above it, glowed in the infernal light. Not so white as the metal pouring from a blast furnace, not so hot, a more sullen red, but welling up from the central primordial fires of the earth. This great pot has boiled over many times in the recent past, as the lava-beds we traveled over testify, and it will probably boil over again. It has been unusually active these last few years.

About nine o'clock we rode back, facing a cold, driving mist, the back of each rider, protected by the shining yellow "slickers," glowing to the one behind him, in the volcano's light, till we were a mile or more away.

The next morning came clear, and the sight of the mighty slope of Mauna Loa, lit up by the rising sun, was a grand spectacle. It looked gentle and easy of ascent, wooded here and there, and here and there showing broad, black streaks from the lava overflows at the summit in recent years; but remembering that it was nearly four thousand feet higher than Haleakala, I had no desire to climb it. This mountain and its companion, Mauna Kea, are the highest island mountains in the world.

39

The stage rolled us back through the fern forest to the railway station and thence on to Hilo again, where in good time, in the afternoon, we went aboard the steamer; and the next morning we were again in the harbor of Honolulu, glad we had made the inter-island trip, and above all glad that we had seen Haleakala.

VI

THE OLD ICE-FLOOD

I

He was a bold man who first conceived the idea of the great continental ice-sheet which in Pleistocene times covered most of the northern part of the continent, and played such a part in shaping the land as we know it. That bold man was Agassiz, who, however, was not bold enough to accept the theory of evolution as propounded by Darwin. The idea of the great glacier did not conflict with Agassiz's religious predilections, and the theory of evolution did. It was a bold generalization, this of the continental ice-sheet, one of the master-strokes of the scientific imagination. It was about the year 1840 that Agassiz, fresh from the glaciers of the Alps, went to Scotland looking for the tracks of the old glaciers, and he found them at once when he landed near Glasgow. We can all find them now on almost every walk we take to the fields and hills; but until our eyes are opened, how blind we are to them! We are like people who camp on the trail of an army and never suspect an army has passed, though the ruts made by their wagons and artillery and the ruins of their intrenchments are everywhere visible.

When I was a boy on the farm we never asked ourselves questions about the stones and rocks that encumbered the land—whence they came, or what the agency was that brought them. The farmers believed the land was created just as we saw it—stones, boulders, soil, gravel-pits, hills, mountains, and all—and doubtless wished in their hearts that the Creator had not been so particular about the rocks and stones, or had made an exception in favor of their own fields. Rocks and stones were good for fences and foundations, and for various other uses, but they were a great hindrance to the cultivation of the soil. I once heard a farmer boast that he had very strong land—it had to be strong to hold up such a crop of rocks and stones. When the Eastern farmer moved west into the prairie states, or south into the cotton-growing states, he probably never asked himself why the Creator had not cumbered the ground with rocks and stones in those sections, as he had in New York and New England. South of the line that runs irregularly through middle New Jersey, Pennsylvania, Ohio, Indiana, Illinois, Iowa, and so on to the Rockies, he will find few loose stones scattered over the soil, no detached boulders sitting upon the surface, no hills or mounds of gravel and sand, no clay banks packed full of rounded stones, little and big, no rocky floors under the soil which look as if they had been dressed down by a huge but dulled and nicked jack-plane. The reason is that the line I have indicated marks the limit of the old ice-sheet which more than a hundred thousand years ago covered all the northern part of the continent to a depth of from two to four thousand feet, and was the chief instrument in rounding off mountain-tops, scattering rock-fragments, little and big, over our landscapes, grinding down and breaking off the protruding rock strata, building up our banks of mingled clay and stone, changing the courses of streams and rivers, deepening and widening our valleys, transplanting boulders of one formation for hundreds of miles, and dropping them upon the surface of another formation. When it began to melt and retreat, it was the chief agent in building up our river terraces, and our long, low, rounded hills of sand and gravel and clay, called kames and drumlins. In many of our valleys its flowing waters left long, low ridges, gentle in outline, made up entirely of sand and gravel, or of clay. In other places it left moraines made up of earth, gravel, and rock-fragments that make a very rough streak through the farmer's land. All those high, level terraces along the Hudson, such as that upon which West Point stands, were the work of the old ice-sheet that once filled the river valley. The melting ice was also the chief agent in building up the enormous clay-banks that are found along the shores of the Hudson. The clay formed in very still waters, the sand and gravel in more active waters.

This great ice-sheet not only covered our northern farms with rocks and stones, and packed the soil with rounded boulders, but it also carried away much of the rock decay that goes to the making of the soil, so that the soil is of greater depth in the non-glaciated than in the glaciated areas of the country. The New-Englander or New-Yorker in traveling in the Southern States may note the enormous depth of soil as revealed by the water-courses or railroad cuts. The ice-sheet was a huge mill that ground up the rocks in the North probably as fast or faster than the rains and the rank vegetation reduced them in the South, but the floods of water which it finally let loose carried a great deal of the rock-waste into the sea.

The glacier milk which colors the streams that flow from beneath it finally settles and makes clay. Off the great Malaspina Glacier in Alaska the ocean is tinged by the glacier milk for nearly fifty miles from the shores. Very few country people, even among the educated, are ready to believe that this enormous ice-sheet ever existed. To make them believe that it is just as much a fact in the physical history of this

40

continent as the war of the Revolution is a fact in our political history is no easy matter. It certainly is a crushing proposition. It so vastly transcends all our experience with ice and snow, or the experience of the race since the dawn of history, that only the scientific imagination and faith are equal to it. The belief in it rests on indubitable evidence, its record is written all over our landscape, but it requires, I say, the scientific imagination to put the facts together and make a continuous history.

Three or four hundred feet above my cabin, five or six hundred feet above tidewater, there is a bold rocky point upon which the old ice-sheet bore heavily. It has rubbed it down and flattened it as a hand passing over a knob of soft putty might do. The great hand in this case moved from the northeast and must have fairly made this rocky prominence groan with its weight. The surface, scratched and grooved and planed by the ice, has weathered away, leaving the rock quite rough; its general outlines alone tell the tale of the battle with the ice. But on the east side a huge mass of rock, that had been planed and gouged by the glacier, was detached and toppled over, turning topsy-turvy before it had weathered, and it lies in such a position, upheld by two rock fragments, that its glaciated surface, though protected from the weather, is clearly visible. You step down two or three feet between the two upholding rocks and are at the entrance of a little cave, and there before you, standing at an angle of thirty or forty degrees, is this rocky page written over with the history of the passing of the great ice plane. The surface exposed is ten or twelve feet long, and four or five feet wide, and it is as straight and smooth, and the scratches and grooves are as sharp and distinct as if made yesterday. I often take the college girls there who come to visit me, to show them, as I tell them, where the old ice gods left their signatures. The girls take turns in stooping down and looking along the under surface of the rock, and feeling it with their hands, and marveling. They have read or heard about these things, but the reading or hearing made little impression upon their minds. When they see a concrete example, and feel it with their hands, they are impressed. Then when I tell them that there is not a shadow of a doubt but that the ice was at one time two or three thousand feet thick above the place where they now stand, and that it bore down upon Julian's Rock with a weight of thousands of tons to the square foot, that it filled all the Hudson River Valley, and covered the landscape for thousands of miles around them, riding over the tops of the Catskills and of the Adirondacks, and wearing them down and carrying fragments of rock torn from them hundreds of miles to the south and southwest,—when I have told them all of this, I have usually given them a mouthful too big for them to masticate or swallow. As a sort of abstract proposition contained in books, or heard in the classroom, they do not mind it, but as an actual fact, here in the light of common day on the hill above Slabsides, with the waters of the Hudson glistening below, and the trees rustling in the wind all about us, that is quite another matter. It sounds like a dream or a fable. Many of the processes that have made our globe what we see it have been so slow and on such a scale that they are quite beyond our horizon— beyond the reach of our mental apprehension. The mind has to approach them slowly and tentatively, and become familiar with the idea of them, before it can give any sort of rational assent to them. It has taken the geologist a long time to work out and clear up and confirm this conception of the great continental glacier which in Pleistocene times covered so large a part of the northern hemisphere. It is now as well established as any event in the remote past well can be. In Alaska, and in the Swiss Alps, one may see the ice doing exactly what the Pleistocene ice-sheet did over this country.

II

The other day in passing a farmer's house I saw where he had placed a huge, roundish boulder, nearly as high as a man's head, by the roadside and had cut upon it his own name and date, and that of his father before him, and that of the first settler upon the farm, in the latter part of the eighteenth century. It was an interesting monument. I learned that the rock had been found in the bed of a small creek near by, and that the farmer had given a hundred dollars to have it moved to its place in front of his house. Had I seen the old farmer I am sure I could have added to his interest and pride in his monument by telling him that it was Adiron-dack gneiss, and had been brought from that region on the back, or in the maw, of a glacier, many tens of thousands of years ago. But it is highly probable that, were he an uneducated man, he would have treated my statement with contempt or incredulity. Education does at least this for a man: it opens his mind and makes him less skeptical about things not dreamed of in his philosophy.

This boulder had been rolled and worn in its long, slow ride till it was nearly round. I have a much smaller boulder, probably from the same quarry, which I planted at the head of my garden for a seat when the hoe gets tired. When it was dropped here on the land that is now my field, the bed and valley of the Hudson were occupied by the old glacier which, during its decline and recession, built up the terraces opposite me (where now stands a multimillionaire's copy of an Italian palace), and which added to and uncovered the river slopes where now my own vineyards are planted.

The flowing or the creeping of this old ice-sheet, so that it could transport large boulders hundreds of miles, is one of the most remarkable things about it: as slow or slower than the hour-hand of the clock, yet an actual progression, carrying it, in the course of thousands of years, from its apex in Labrador well down into New Jersey, where its terminal moraine is still clearly traceable.

A river of ice, under the right conditions, flows as literally as a river of water, fastest in the middle, and slowest along its margins where the friction is greatest. The old ice-sheet, or ice sea, flowed around and over mountains as a river flows around and over rocks. Where a mountain rose above the glacier, the ice divided and flowed round it, and reunited again beyond it. One may see all this in Alaska at the present time. Water, of course, flows because of its own pressure; so does ice, only the pressure has to be vastly greater. A drop of water on the table does not flow, but, pile it high enough, and it will. The old ice sea flowed mainly south, not because it was downhill in that direction, but because the accumulation of ice and snow at the North was so great. If through any climatic changes, the snowfall were ever again to be so great that more snow should fall in winter than could melt in summer, after the lapse of thousands of years, we should have another ice age.

VII

THE FRIENDLY SOIL

I never tire of contemplating the soil itself, the mantle rock, as the geologist calls it. It clothes the rocky framework of the earth as the flesh clothes our bones. It is the seat of the vitality of the globe, the youngest part, the growing, changing part. Out of it we came, and to it we return. It is literally our mother, as the sun is our father.

The soil!—the residuum of the rocks, the ashes of the mountains. We know what a vast stretch of time has gone to the making of it; that it has been baked and boiled and frozen and thawed, acted upon by sun and star and wind and rain; mixed and remixed and kneaded and added to, as the housewife kneads and moulds her bread; that it has lain under the seas in the stratified rocks for incalculable ages; that chemical and mechanical and vital forces have all had a hand in its preparation; that the vast cycles of animal and vegetable life of the foreworld have contributed to its fertility; that the life of the sea, and the monsters of the earth, and the dragons of the air, have left their ashes here, so that when I stir it with my hoe, or turn it with my spade, I know I am stirring or turning the meal of a veritable grist of the gods.

From its primal source in the Archaean rock, up through all the vast series of sedimentary rocks to our own time, what vicissitudes and transformations it has passed through; how many times it has died, so to speak, and been reborn from the rocks; how many times the winds and the rains have transported it, and infused invisible, life-giving gases into it; how many of the elements have throbbed with life, climbed and bloomed in trees, walked or flown or swam in animals, or slumbered for thousands upon thousands of years beneath the great ice-sheet of Pleistocene time! A handful of the soil by your door is probably the most composite thing you can find in a day's journey. It may be an epitome of a whole geological formation, or of two or more of them. If it happens to be made up of decomposed limestone, sandstone, slate, and basalt rock, think what a history would be condensed in it!

Our lawns are made up of ashes from the funeral pyre of mountains, of dust from the tombs of geologic ages. What masses of rock does this sandbank represent! what an enormous grist in the great glacier mill do these layers of clay stand for! Two feet of soil probably represent a hundred feet or more of rock. Strictly speaking, the soil is the insoluble parts of the ground-up and decomposed rocks, after the rains and the winds have done their work and taken their toll of the grist they have ground. Sometimes these mills take the whole grist and leave the rocks bare; but usually they leave a residuum in which life strikes its roots. We do not see all that the waters take from the soil. They have invisible pockets in which they carry away all the more soluble parts, such as lime, soda, potash, silica, magnesia, and others, and leave for the land the more insoluble parts. These, too, in times of flood they carry away in suspension, in the shape of sand, silt, mud, gravel, and the like. When the waters really digest the rocks, they hold the various minerals in solution, and run limpid and dancing to the sea; when they have an undigested burden, they run angry and turbid.

It is estimated that the Hudson River deposits in the sea each year four hundred and forty thousand tons of mineral matter in solution which it has taken from the land, and the Mississippi one hundred and twelve million tons. Each carries away about four times as much in suspension. The digestive or chemical power of water, then, is only about one fourth as great as its mechanical power. Between the two the land is made to pay heavy toll to the sea. But in time, in geologic time, it all comes back. The suspended particles are dropped and go to make up the sedimentary rocks, while the solutes help cement the material of these rocks together, and also nourish the sea life from which limestone and other organic rocks are made. When these rocks are again lifted to the surface and disintegrated into soil, then the debt of the sea to the land is paid. This process, this cycle of soil loss and soil growth, has gone on through all time, and must continue as long as the rain continues to fall, or as long as the sea continues to send its tax-gatherers to the land. In this great cycle of give and take of the elements, the affairs of men

42

cut but a momentary figure; how puny they are, how transient! How the great changes, which in time amount to revolutions, go on over our heads and under our feet, and we rarely heed them, and are powerless to stay them! A summer shower carries the soil of my side-hill, which is mainly disintegrated Silurian rock and shale, into the river, and some millions of years hence, when it has become stratified rock, and been lifted up into the light of day, some other, and, I trust, wiser husbandman, will be gathering his harvest from it, and be worried over the downpour that robs him of it. The farmer's worry is bound to come back with the soil, and be passed along with it.

VIII

PRIMAL ENERGIES

How puny and meagre is the utmost power man can put forth, even by the aid of all his mechanical appliances, when compared with the primal earth forces! Think, or try to think, of the force of pressure that causes the rock-strata to buckle or crumple or bend—layers of rock, thousands of feet thick, made to fold and bend like the leaves of a book—vast mountain-chains flexed and foreshortened, or ruptured and faulted as the bending of one's body wrinkles or rips one's clothes. Think of the over-thrusts and the folding and shearing of the earth's crust. The shrinking of the earth squeezes the rocks to an extent quite beyond our power of conception. "So overpowering has been the horizontal movement in some cases," says Dana, "that masses of rock thousands of feet in thickness have been buckled up and sheared, or, simply yielding to pressure, have sheared without folding, and been thrust forward for miles along a gently inclined plane. These great reversed faults are termed over-thrusts or thrust-planes. Sometimes such thrust-planes occur singly, at other times the rocks have yielded again and again, great sheets having been sliced off successively, and driven forward one upon the other." In northern Montana there is an over-thrust of the Cambrian rocks upon the late Cretaceous, of seven or eight miles, carrying with it what is now called "Chief Mountain," which has been carved out of the extreme end of the over-thrust. The contemplation of such things gives one a sense of power in Nature beyond anything else I know of. The shrinking of the globe as a whole makes its rocky garment too big for it, and this titanic wrinkling and folding results. When the strata snap asunder under the strain, we have earthquakes. During the recent San Francisco earthquake, Mount Tamalpais, across the bay, and all the neighboring heights, were permanently shifted eight or ten feet. The sides of the mountain, it is said, undulated like a curtain. And this shaking and twitching of the great rocky skin of the earth was vastly less, in proportion to the size of the globe, than the twitching and trembling of the skin of a horse when he would shake off the flies, in comparison with the animal's body.

We see another exhibition of the magnitude of the earth's forces in what the geologist calls a "laccolite"—a great cave or cistern deep beneath the surface of stratified rock filled with hardened lava. The lava is forced up from an unknown depth under such pressure that, not finding an outlet at the surface, the rock strata, hundreds or thousands of feet thick, are lifted up and arched like so much paper, and in the cavity thus formed the pent-up molten lava finds relief. These lava cisterns or pockets are sometimes uncovered by the process of erosion. The Henry Mountains in Utah are all laccolites. One of them, Mount Hillers, has a volume of about ten cubic miles. Much of the overarching sedimentary strata still covers it. Geologists read the evidence of a similar formation called a "sill" on the west side of the Hudson in New Jersey, forming the Palisades. The lava worked like a giant mole up through and then beneath the Triassic sandstone, lifting the strata up and arching them over a large area. During the millions of years that have elapsed since that time, the layers of superincumbent sandstone have been worn away so that now one sees a wide, smooth, gentle slope of basaltic rock covered by a very thin coat of soil. As one goes by on the train, one sees where the workmen of a stone-crushing plant have cut into the slope and uncovered the junction of the two kinds of rock, one born of water, and one born of fire. The igneous rock sits squarely upon the level sandstone, like a row of upright books standing upon a shelf. I never pass the place but that I want to stop the train and get out and have a close look at the precise spot where this son of Vulcan sat down so heavily and so hot upon his brother of the sedimentary deposits.

Probably no two chapters of the earth's history differ more than those of the two sides of the Hudson at New York. There is a great break here—a leap from Archaean times on the east side to Mesozoic times on the west. The east side is millions of years the older. Here is the original Plutonic or Azoic rock which apparently has never been under the sea since it was first thrust up out of the fiery depths. The west shore, including the Palisades, belongs to a much later geologic era. The original granite here is buried under vast deposits of sedimentary rock of the Triassic age—the age of the giant reptiles, the remains of one of which has recently been found embedded in this sandstone, near the river's edge. As the traveler's eye follows along the even, almost level line of this escarpment of the Palisades, let it re-create for him the strata of the old Triassic sandstone that were millions of years ago piled high upon it,—

43

how high can only be conjectured,—but which have been removed grain by grain under the eroding power of the forces of air and water that now seem to caress the huge wall so gently. Ah! geologic Time, what can it not do? what has it not done? The old sill of Vulcan now presents a nearly vertical front to the Hudson, forming the Palisades, showing that some leaves of the earth's history here are missing, buried probably beneath the waters of the river. There is evidently a line of fault here, and the west side has been lifted up out of the old Mesozoic seas, probably in the convulsions that poured out the lava of the trap rock.

IX
SCIENTIFIC FAITH

I find myself accepting certain things on the authority of science which so far transcend my experience, and the experience of the race and all the knowledge of the world, in fact which come so near being unthinkable, that I call my acceptance of them an act of scientific faith. One's reason may be convinced and yet the heart refuse to believe. It is not so much a question of evidence as a question of capacity to receive evidence of an unusual kind.

One of the conclusions of science which I feel forced to accept, and yet which I find very hard work to believe, is that of the animal origin of man. I suppose my logical faculties are convinced, but what is that in me that is baffled, and that hesitates and demurs?

The idea of the origin of man from some lower form requires such a plunge into the past, and such a faith in the transforming power of the biological laws, and in the divinity that lurks in the soil underfoot and streams from the orbs overhead, that the ordinary mind is quite unequal to the task. For the book of Genesis of the old Bible we have substituted the book of genesis of the rocky scripture of the globe—a book torn and mutilated, that has been through fire and flood and earthquake shock, that has been in the sea and on the heights, and that only the palaeontologist can read or decipher correctly, but which is a veritable bible of the succession of life on the earth. The events of the days of creation are recorded here, but they are days of such length that they are to be reckoned only in millions of years.

The evolution of the horse, according to the best and latest research, from the eohippus of Eocene times—a small mammal no larger than the fox—to the proud and fleet creature that we prize to-day, occupied four or five millions of years. Think of that first known progenitor of the horse as never dying, but living on through the geological ages and being slowly, oh, so slowly, modified by its environment, changing its teeth, its hoofs, enlarging its body, lengthening its limbs, and so on, till it becomes the horse we know to-day.

In accepting the theory of the animal origin of man we have got to follow man back, not only till we find him a naked savage like the Fuegians as Darwin describes them,—naked, bedaubed with paint, with matted hair and looks wild and distrustful,—but we cannot stop there, we must follow him back till he becomes a troglodyte, a cave-dweller, contending with the cave bear, the cave lion, and the hyena for the possession of this rude shelter; back still, till we find him in trees living like the anthropoid apes; then back to the earth again to some four-footed creature, probably of the marsupial kind; still the trail leads downward and ever downward, till we lose it in that maze of marine forms that swarm in the Palaeozoic seas, or until the imagination is baffled and refuses to proceed. It certainly is a hard proposition, and it puts one upon his mettle to accept it.

Should we not find equal difficulty in believing the life-history of each one of us,—the start in the germ, then the vague suggestion of fish, and frog, and reptile, in our foetal life,—were it not a matter of daily experience? Let it be granted that the race of man was born as literally out of the animal forms below him as the child is born out of these vague, prenatal animal forms in its mother's womb. Yet the former fact so far transcends our experience, and even our power of imagination, that we can receive it only by an act of scientific faith, as our fathers received the dogmas of the Church by an act of religious faith.

I confess that I find it hard work to get on intimate terms with evolution, familiarize my mind with it, and make it thinkable. The gulf that separates man from the orders below him is so impassable, his intelligence is so radically different from theirs, and his progress so enormous, while they have stood still, that believing it is like believing a miracle. That the apparently blind groping and experimentation which mark the course of evolution as revealed by palaeontology—the waste, the delay, the vicissitudes, the hit-and-miss method—should have finally resulted in this supreme animal, man, puts our scientific faith to the test. In the light of evolution how the halo with which we have surrounded our origin vanishes!

Man has from the earliest period believed himself of divine origin, and by the divine he has meant something far removed from this earth and all its laws and processes, something quite transcending the mundane forces. He has invented or dreamed myths and legends to throw the halo of the exceptional, the far removed, the mystical, or the divine around his origin. He has spurned the clod with his foot; he has

44

denied all kinship with bird and beast around him, and looked to the heavens above for the sources of his life. And then unpitying science comes along and tells him that he is under the same law as the life he treads under foot, and that that law is adequate to transform the worm into the man; that he, too, has groveled in the dust, or wallowed in the slime, or fought and reveled, a reptile among reptiles; that the heavens above him, to which he turns with such awe and reverence, or such dread and foreboding, are the source of his life and hope in no other sense than they are the source of the life and hope of all other creatures. But this is the way of science; it enhances the value or significance of everything about us that we are wont to treat as cheap or vulgar, and it discounts the value of the things far off upon which we have laid such stress. It ties us to the earth, it calls in the messengers we send forth into the unknown; it makes the astonishing revelation— revolutionary revelation, I may say—that the earth is embosomed in the infinite heavens the same as the stars that shine above us, that the creative energy is working now and here underfoot, the same as in the ages of myth and miracle; in other words, that God is really immanent in his universe, and inseparable from it; that we have been in heaven and under the celestial laws all our lives, and knew it not. Science thus kills religion, poetry, and romance only so far as it dispels our illusions and brings us back from the imaginary to the common and the near at hand. It discounts heaven in favor of earth. It should make us more at home in the world, and more conscious of the daily beauty and wonders that surround us, and, if it does not, the trouble is probably in the ages of myth and fable that lie behind us and that have left their intoxicating influence in our blood.

We are willing to be made out of the dust of the earth when God makes us, the God we have made ourselves out of our dreams and fears and aspirations, but we are not willing to be made out of the dust of the earth when the god called Evolution makes us. An impersonal law or process we cannot revere or fear or worship or exalt; we can only study it and put it to the test. We can love or worship only personality. This is why science puts such a damper upon us; it banishes personality, as we have heretofore conceived it, from the universe. The thunder is no longer the voice of God, the earth is no longer his footstool. Personality appears only in man; the universe is not inhuman, but unhuman. It is this discovery that we recoil from, and blame science for; and until, in the process of time, we shall have adjusted our minds, and especially our emotions, to it, mankind will still recoil from it.

We love our dreams, our imaginings, as we love a prospect before our houses. We love an outlook into the ideal, the unknown in our lives. But we love also to feel the solid ground beneath our feet.

Whether life loses in charm as we lose our illusions, and whether it gains in power and satisfaction as we more and more reach solid ground in our beliefs, is a question that will be answered differently by different persons.

We have vastly more solid knowledge about the universe amid which we live than had our fathers, but are we happier, better, stronger? May it not be said that our lives consist, not in the number of things we know any more than in the number of things we possess, but in the things we love, in the depth and sincerity of our emotions, and in the elevation of our aspirations? Has not science also enlarged the sphere of our love, and given us new grounds for wonder and admiration? It certainly has, but it as certainly has put a damper upon our awe, our reverence, our veneration. However valuable these emotions are, and whatever part they may have played in the development of character in the past, they seem doomed to play less and less part in the future. Poetry and religion, so called, seem doomed to play less and less part in the life of the race in the future. We shall still dream and aspire, but we shall not tremble and worship as in the past.

We see about us daily transformations as stupendous as that of the evolution of man from the lower animals, and we marvel not. We see the inorganic pass into the organic, we see iron and lime and potash and silex blush in the flowers, sweeten in the fruit, ripen in the grain, crimson in the blood, and we marvel not. We see the spotless pond-lily rising and unfolding its snowy petals, and its trembling heart of gold, from the black slime of the pond. We contemplate our own life-history as shown in our pre-natal life, and we are not disturbed. But when we stretch this process out through the geologic ages and try to see ourselves a germ, a fish, a reptile, in the womb of time, we are balked. We do not see the great mother, or the great father, or feel the lift of the great biologic laws. We are beyond our depth. It is easy to believe that the baby is born of woman, because it is a matter of daily experience, but it is not easy to believe that man is born of the animal world below him, and that that is born of inorganic Nature, because the fact is too big and tremendous.

What we call Nature works in no other way; one law is over big and little alike. What Nature does in a day typifies what she does in an eternity. It is when we reach the things done on such an enormous scale of time and power and size that we are helpless. The almost infinitely slow transformations that the theory of evolution demands balk us as do the size and distance of the fixed stars.

No observation or study of evolution on a small scale and near at hand in the familiar facts of the life about us can prepare us for it, any more than lake and river can prepare us for the ocean, or the modeling of miniature valleys and mountains by the rain in the clay bank can open our minds to receive the tremendous facts of the carving of the face of the continent by the same agents.

We do not see evolution working in one day, or in a century, or in many centuries. Neither do we catch the gods of erosion at their Herculean tasks. They always seem to be having a holiday, or else to be merely toying with their work.

When we see a mound of earth or a bank of clay worn into miniature mountain-chains and canons and gulches by the rains of a season, we do not doubt our eyes; we know the rains did it. But when we see the same thing copied in a broad landscape, or on the face of a state or a continent, we find it hard to believe the evidence of our own senses. The scale upon which it is done, and the time involved, put it so far beyond the sphere of our experience that something in us, probably the practical, everyday man, refuses to be convinced.

The lay mind can hardly have any adequate conception of the part erosion, the simple weathering of the rocks, has played in shaping our landscapes, and in preparing the earth for the abode of man. The changes in the surface of the land in one's lifetime, or even in the historic period, are so slight that the tales the geologists tell us are incredible.

When, during a recent trip through the great Southwest, I saw the earth laid open by erosion as I had never before dreamed of, especially when I visited those halls of the gods, the Grand Canon and Yosemite Valley, I found my capacity to believe in the erosive power of water and the weather quite overtaxed. It must be true, I said, what the geologists tell us, that water and air did all this; but while you look and wait, and while generations before you have looked and waited, all is as quiet and passive as if the slumber of ages wrapped hill and vale. Invisible giants have wrought and delved here of whom we never catch a glimpse, nor shall we, wait and watch we never so long. No sound of their hammers or picks or shovels or of the dynamite ever breaks the stillness of the air.

I have to believe that the valleys and mountains of my native Catskills were carved out of a great elevated plain or plateau; there is no other explanation of them. Here lie the level strata, without any bending or folding, or sign of convulsion and upheavals, horizontal as the surface of the sea or lake in which their sediments were originally laid down; and here are these deep, wide valleys cut down through these many sheets of stratified rock; and here are these long, high, broad-backed mountains, made up of the rock that the forces of air and water have left, and with no forces of erosion at work that would appreciably alter a line of the landscape in ten thousand years; and yet we know, if we know anything about the physical history of the earth, that erosion has done this work, carved out these mountains and valleys, from the Devonian strata, as literally as the sculptor carves his statue from the block of marble.

Above my lodge on the home farm the vast layers of the gray, thin-sheeted Catskill rock crop out and look across the valley to their fellows two or more miles away where they crop out in a similar manner on the opposite slope of the mountain. With the eye of faith I see the great sheets restored, and follow them across on the line which they made aeons ago, till they are joined again to their fellows as they were before the agents of erosion had so widely severed them.

These physical forces have worked as slowly and silently in sculpturing the landscapes as the biological laws have worked in evolving man from the lower animals, or the vertebrates from the invertebrates. The rains, the dews, the snows, the winds—how could these soft, gently careering agents have demolished these rocks and dug these valleys? One would almost as soon expect the wings and feet of the birds to wear away the forests they flit through. The wings of time are feathered also, and as they brush against the granite or the flinty sandstone no visible particle is removed while you watch and wait. Come back in a thousand years, and you note no change, save in the covering of trees and verdure. Return in ten thousand, and you would probably find the hills carrying their heads as high and as proudly as ever. Here and there the face of the cliff may have given way, or a talus slid into the valley, or a stream or river changed its course, or sawed deeper into the rock, and a lake been turned into a marsh, or the delta of a river broadened—minor changes, such as a shingle from your roof or a brick from your chimney, while your house stands as before. In one hundred thousand years what changes should we probably find? Here in the Catskills, where I write, the weathering of the hills and mountains would probably have been but slight. It must be fifty thousand years or more since the great ice-sheet left us. Where protected by a thin coat of soil, its scratches and grooves upon the surface rock are about as fresh and distinct as you may see them made in Alaska at the present time. Where the rock is exposed, they have weathered out, one eighth of an inch probably having been worn away. The drifting of the withered leaves of autumn, or of the snows of winter over them, it really seems, would have done as much in that stretch of time. Then try to fancy the eternity it has taken the subaerial elements to cut thousands of feet through this hard Catskill sandstone! No, the evolution of the landscape, the evolution of the animal and vegetable kingdoms, the evolution of the suns and planets, involve a process so slow, and on such a scale, that it is quite unthinkable. How long it took evolution to bridge the chasm between the vertebrate and the invertebrate, between the fish and the frog, between the frog and the reptile, between the reptile and the mammal, or between the lowest mammal and the highest, who can guess?

But the gulf has been passed, and here we are in this teeming world of life and beauty, with a terrible past behind us, but a brighter and brighter future before us.

X

"THE WORM STRIVING TO BE MAN"

When our minds have expanded sufficiently to take in and accept the theory of evolution, with what different feelings we look upon the visible universe from those with which our fathers looked upon it! Evolution makes the universe alive. In its light we see that mysterious potency of matter itself, that something in the clod under foot that justifies Emerson's audacious line of the "worm striving to be man." We are no longer the adopted children of the earth, but her own real offspring. Evolution puts astronomy and geology in our blood and authenticates us and gives us the backing of the whole solar system. This is the redemption of the earth: it is the spiritualization of matter.

In imagination stand off in vacant space and see the earth rolling by you, a huge bubble with all its continents and seas and changing seasons and countless forms of life upon it, and remember that you are looking upon a great cosmic organism, pulsing with the vital currents of the universe, and that what it holds of living forms were not arbitrarily imposed upon it from without, but vitally evolved from within and that man himself is one of its products as literally as are the trees that stand rooted to the soil. Revert to the time when life was not, when the globe was a half-incandescent ball, or when it was a seething, weltering waste of heated water, before the land had yet emerged from the waves, and yet you and I were there in the latent potencies of the chemically and dynamically warring elements. We were there, the same as the heat and flame are in the coal and wood and as the explosive force of powder is in the grains. The creative cosmic chemistry in due time brought us forth, and started us on the long road that led from the amoeba up to man. There have been no days of creation. Creation has been a continuous process, and the creator has been this principle of evolution inherent in all matter.

Man himself was born of this principle. His genealogy finally runs back to the clod under his feet. One has no trouble in accepting the old Biblical account of his origin from the dust of the earth when one views that dust in the light of modern science.

Man is undoubtedly of animal origin. He is embraced in the same zoological scheme as are all other creatures, and did not start as man any more than you and I started with our present stature, or than the earth sprang from chaos as we now behold it.

His complete physical evolution must have been achieved thousands of centuries ago, but his full mental and spiritual evolution is not yet.

I think of his physical evolution as completed when he assumed the upright attitude or passed from a quadruped to a biped, which must of itself have been a long, slow process. Probably our whole historic period would form but a fraction of this cycle of unrecorded time. Man's complete emergence from the lower orders, so that he stood off in sharp contrast to them in his physical form probably occurred in later Tertiary times, and what the meaning of this stretch of time is in human years we can only conjecture. During this cycle of numberless millenniums till the dawn of history, man's development was mainly mental. He left the brute creature behind because his mind continued to develop after his physical form was complete, while the brute stood still. Whence the impulse that sent man forward? Why was one animal form endowed with the capacity for endless growth and development, and all the others denied it? Ah! that is the question of questions. Compared with the development of his bodily powers, man's mental and spiritual growth has been very rapid. He seems to have been millions of years in getting his body, while he has been only millenniums in getting his reason and intelligence. What progress since the dawn of history! Compare the Germans of the time of Tacitus, or the Gauls of the time of Caesar, or the Britons of the time of Hadrian with the people of those countries to-day.

We are prone to speak of man's emergence from the lower orders as if it were a simple thing, almost like the going from one country into another. But try to think what it means; try to think of the slow transformation, of the long, toilsome road even from the halfway house of our simian ancestors. If we do not give him the benefit of the sudden mutation theory of the origin of species, then think of the slow process, hair by hair, as it were, by which a tailed, apelike arboreal animal was transformed into a hairless, tailless, erect, tool-using, fire-using, speech-forming animal. We see in our own day in the case of the African negro, that centuries of our Northern climate have hardly any appreciable effect toward making a white man of him; nor, on the other hand, has exposure to the tropical sun had much more effect in making a negro of the white man. Probably it would take ten thousand years or more of these conditions to bleach the pigments out of the one skin and put them in the other. There is convincing proof from painting and figures found in Egypt that neither the African negro nor the Egyptian has changed in features in five thousand years.

The most marvelous thing about man's evolution is the inborn upward impulse in some one low organism that rested not till it reached its goal in him. The mollusk remains, but some impulse went out from the mollusk that begat the fish. The fish remains, but some impulse went out from the fish that begat the amphibian. The amphibian remains, but some impulse went out from the amphibian that begat the reptile. The reptile remains, but some impulse went out from the reptile that begat the mammal; and so on up to man. Man must have had a specific line of descent. One golden thread must connect him with the lowest forms of life. And the wonder is that this golden thread was never snapped or lost through all the terrible vicissitudes of the geologic ages. But I suppose it is just as great a wonder that the line of descent of the horse, or the sheep, or the dog, or the bird, was not snapped or lost. Some impulse or tendency was latent or potential in the first unicellular life that rested not till it eventuated in each of these higher forms. Did any terrestrial or celestial calamity endanger the line of descent of any of the higher creatures? Was any form cut off in the world-wide crustal disturbances of the earth at the end of palaeozoic and mesozoic time, when so many forms of animal life appear to have been wiped out, that might in time have given birth to a kind unlike or superior to any now upon the earth? Species after species have become extinct, whole orders and families have gone out, often rather suddenly. Why we know not. Why the line of man's descent was not cut off, who knows? It is a vain speculation. There can be little doubt that in early Tertiary times our ancestor was a small, feeble mammal, maybe of the lemur, maybe of the marsupial kind, powerless before the great carnivorous mammals of that time, and probably escaping them by his greater agility, perhaps by his arboreal habits. The ancestor of the horse was also a small creature at that time, not larger than a fox. It was not cut off; the line of descent seems complete to the horse of our day. Small beginnings seem to be the rule in all provinces of life. There is little doubt that the great animals of our day—the elephant, the whale, the lion,—all had their start in small forms. Many of these small forms have been found. But a complete series of any of the animal forms that eventuated in any of the dominant species is yet wanting. It is quite certain that the huge, the gigantic, the monstrous in animal, as in vegetable life, lies far behind us. Is it not quite certain that evolution in the life of the globe has run its course, and that it will not again bring forth reptiles or mammals of the terrible proportions of those of past geologic ages? nor ferns, nor mosses, nor as gigantic trees as those of Carboniferous times? Probably the redwoods of the Far West, the gigantic sequoias, are the last race of gigantic trees. The tide of life of the globe is undoubtedly at the full. The flood has no doubt been checked many times. The glacial periods, of which there seem to have been several in different parts of the earth, and in different geological periods, no doubt checked it when it occurred. But the tide as a whole must have steadily risen, because the progression from lower to higher forms has gone steadily forward. The lower forms have come along; Nature has left nothing behind. The radiates, the articulates, the mollusca, are still with us, but in the midst of these the higher and higher forms have been constantly appearing. The great biological tree has got its growth. Many branches and twigs have died and dropped off, and many more will do so, are doing so before our eyes, but I cannot help doubting that any new branches of importance are yet to appear—any new families or orders of birds, or fishes, or reptiles, or mammals. The horse, the stag, the sheep, the dog, the cat, as we know them, are doubtless the end of the series. One arrives at this conclusion upon general principles. Life as a whole must run its course or reach its high-water mark, the same as life in its particular phases. Man has arrived and has universal dominion; all things are put under his feet. The destiny of life upon the globe is henceforth largely in his hands. Not even he can avert the final cosmic catastrophe which physicists foresee, and which, according to Professor Lowell, the beings upon Mars are now struggling to ward off.

Man has taken his chances in the clash of forces of the physical universe. No favor has been shown him, or is shown him to-day, and yet he has come to his estate. He has never been coddled; fire, water, frost, gravity, hunger, death, have made and still make no exceptions in his favor. He is on a level with all other animals in this respect. He has his life and well-being on the same terms as do the fowls of the air and the beasts of the fields.

Archbishop Whately thought that primitive man could never have raised himself to a higher condition without external aid—some "elementary instruction to enable his faculties to begin their work." He must have had a boost. Well, the boost was forthcoming, but it was not from without, but from within, through this principle of development, this upward striving that was innate from the first in certain forms of life and of which Whately had no conception. It was the conception of his time that creation was like a watch made and wound up by some power external to itself.

48

The physical evolution of man, as I have said, is no doubt complete. He will never have wings, or more legs, or longer arms, or a bigger brain. The wings and the extra legs and the keener sense he has left behind him. His development henceforth must be in the mental and spiritual. He is bound to have more and more dominion over Nature, and see more and more clearly his own relation to her. He will in time completely subdue and possess the earth. Yes, and probably exhaust her? But he will see in time that he is squandering his inheritance and will mend his ways. He will conserve in the future as he has wasted in the past. He will learn to conserve his own health. He will banish disease; he will stamp out all the plagues and scourges, through his scientific knowledge; he will double or treble the length of life. Man has undoubtedly passed through and finished certain phases of his emotional and mental development. He will never again be the religious enthusiast and fanatic he has been in the past; he has not worshiped his last, but he has worshiped his best. He will build no more cathedrals; he will burn no more martyrs at the stake. His religion as such is on the wane. But his humanitarianism is a rising tide. He is becoming less and less a savage, revolts more and more at the sight of blood and suffering. The highly religious ages were ages of blood and persecution. Man's tenderness for man has vastly increased. The sense of the sacredness of human life has increased as his faith in his gods has declined. He has grown more human as he has grown less superstitious. Science has atrophied his faith, but it has softened his heart. His fear of Nature has given place to love. Man never loved as he does now. He has withdrawn his gaze from heaven and fixed it upon the earth. As his interest in other worlds has diminished, his interest in this has increased. As the angels have departed, the children have come in.

When the nations, too, cease to be savage and selfish, and become altruistic, then the new birth of humanity will actually have occurred. As an artist and a creator of beautiful forms, man has also had his day; he loved the beautiful, the artistic, or the ornamental long before he loved the true and the just. He was proud before he was kind; he was chivalrous before he was decent; he was tattooed before he was washed; he was painted before he was clothed; he built temples before he built a home; he sacrificed to his gods before he helped his neighbor; he was heroic before he was self-denying; he was devout before he was charitable. We are losing the savage virtues and vanities and growing in the grace of all the humanities, and this process will doubtless go on, with many interruptions and setbacks of course, till the kingdom of love is at last fairly established upon the earth.

XI
THE PHANTOMS BEHIND US
I

I take the title of this paper from those great lines in Whitman beginning—
"Rise after rise bow the phantoms behind me"—
in which he launches in vivid imaginative form the whole doctrine of evolution some years before Darwin had published his epoch-making work on the "Origin of Species."
"I see afar down the huge first Nothing, and I know I was even there."
I do not know that Whitman had any concrete belief in the truth of the animal origin of man. He read as picture and parable that which the man of science reads as demonstrable fact. He saw and felt the great truth of evolution, but he saw it as written in his own heart and not in the great stone book of the earth, and he saw it written large. He felt its cosmic truth, its truth in relation to the whole scheme of things; he felt his own kinship with all that lives, and had a vivid personal sense of his debt to the past, not only of human history, but also to the past of the earth and the spheres. And he felt this as a poet and not as a man of science.

The theory of evolution as applied to the whole universe and its inevitable corollary, the animal origin of man, is now well established in most of the leading minds of the world, but it is still rejected by many timid and sensitive souls, and it will be a long time before it becomes universally accepted.

Doubtless one source of the trouble we have in accepting the theory comes from the fact that our minds have not been used to such thoughts; in the mind of the race they are a new thing: they are not in the literature nor in the philosophy nor in the sacred books in which our minds have been nurtured; they are of yesterday; they came to us raw and unhallowed by the usage of ages; more than that, they savor of the materialism of all modern science, which is so distasteful to our finer ideals and religious sensibilities. In fact, these ideas are strangers of an alien race in our intellectual household, and we look upon them coldly and distrustfully. But probably to our children, or to our children's children, they will wear quite a different countenance; they will have become an accepted part of the great family of ideas of the race.

Another hindrance is the dullness and opacity of our own minds. We are slow to wake up to a sense of the divinity that hedges us about. The great office of science has been to show us this universe as much more wonderful and divine than we have been wont to believe; shot through and through with celestial laws and forces; matter, indeed, but matter informed with spirit and intelligence; the creative energy inherent and active in the ground underfoot not less than in the stars and nebulae overhead.

We look for the divine afar off. We gaze upon the beauty and purity of the heavenly bodies without thinking that we are also in the heavens. We must open our minds to the stupendous fact that God is immanent in his universe and that it is literally and exactly true, as we were taught long ago, that, during every moment of our lives, in Him we live and move and have our being.

Moreover, we are staggered by the element of vast time that is implied in the history of development. Were it not for the records in the rocks, we could not believe it at all. All the grand movements and processes of nature are quite beyond our ken. In the heavens only the astronomer with his prisms and telescopes traces them; only the geologist and palaeontologist read their history in the earth's crust. The soil we cultivate was once solid rock, but not in one lifetime, not in many lifetimes, do we see the transformation of the rocks into soil. Nations may rise and fall, and the rocks they looked upon and the soil they tilled remain practically unchanged. Geologists talk about the ancient continents that have passed away. What an abyss of time such things open! They talk about the birth of a mountain or the decay of a mountain as we talk of the birth and death of a man, but in doing so they reckon with periods of time for which we have no standards of measurement. They walk and talk with the Eternal. To us the mountains seem as fixed as the stars. But the stars, too, are flitting. Look at Orion some millions of years hence, and he will have been torn limb from limb. The combination of stars that forms that striking constellation and all other constellations is temporary as the grouping of the clouds. The rise of man from the lower orders implies a scale of time almost as great. It is unintelligible to us because it belongs to a category of facts that transcends our experience and the experience of the race as the interstellar spaces transcend our earthly measurements.

We now gaze upon the order below us across an impassable gulf, but that gulf we have crossed and without any supernatural means of transportation. We may say it has been bridged or filled with the humble ancestral forms that carried forward the precious evolutionary impulse of the vertebrate series till it culminated in man. All vestiges of that living bridge are now gone, and the legend of our crossing seems like a dream or a miracle. Biological evolution has gone hand in hand with geological evolution, and both are on a scale of time of which our hour-glass of the centuries gives us but a faint hint. Our notions of time are not formed on the pattern of the cosmic processes, or the geologic processes, or the evolutionary processes; they are formed on the pattern of our own brief span of life. In a few cases in the familiar life about us we see the evolutionary process abridged, and transformations like those of unrecorded time take place before our eyes, as when the tadpole becomes the frog or the grub becomes the butterfly. These rapid changes are analogous to those which in the depths of geologic time have evolved the bird from the fish or the reptile, or the seal and the manatee from a fourfooted land animal. Our common bluebird has long been recognized as a descendant of the thrush family; this origin is evident in the speckled breast of the young birds and in the voices of the mature birds. I have heard a bluebird with an unmistakable thrush note. The transformation has doubtless been so slow that an analogous change taking place in any of the bird forms of our own time would entirely escape observation. The bluebird may have been as long in getting his blue coat as man has been in getting his upright position.

Looking into the laws and processes of the common nature about us for clues to the origin of man is not unlike looking into the records of the phonograph for the secret of the music which that wonderful instrument voices for us. Something, some active principle or agent, has to invoke the music that slumbers or is latent in these lines.

In like manner some principle or force that we do not see is active in the ground underfoot and in the forms of life about us which is the final secret of the origin of man and of all other creatures. This something is the evolutionary impulse, this innate aspiration of living matter to reach higher and higher forms. "Urge and urge," says Whitman, "always the procreant urge of the world." It is in Emerson's worm "striving to be man." This "striving" pervades organic nature. Whence its origin science does not assume to say. [Footnote: This passage was written long before I had read Bergson's Creative Evolution, as were several others of the same import in this volume.]

Then the difference in kind between the mind of man and that of the lower orders makes evolution a doubly hard problem.

Look over the globe and see what a gulf separates man from all other creatures. All the other animals seem akin—as if the product of the same workman. Man, in contrast, seems like an introduction from some other sphere or the outcome of quite other psychological laws; his dominion over them all is so complete and universal. Without their specialization of structure or powers, he yet masters them all and uses them; without their powers of speed, he yet outstrips them; without their strength of tusk and limb, he yet subdues them; without their inerrant instinct, he yet outwits them; without their keenness of eye, ear, and nose, he yet wins in the chase; without their special adaptation to environment, he survives when they perish. A man is marked off from the animals below him, I say, as if he were a being of another sphere. He looks into their eyes and they into his, and no recognition passes; and yet we have to believe that he and they are fruit of the same biologic tree and that their stem forms unite in the same trunk somewhere in the abyss of biologic time.

The rise of man from the lower orders taxes our powers of belief and our faith in the divinity that lurks underfoot far more than did the special creation myth. Creation by omnipotent fiat seems easy when you have the omnipotent being to begin with, but creation through evolution is a kind of cosmic or biologic legerdemain that baffles and bewilders us. It so far transcends all our earthly knowledge and experience and all the flights of our philosophy that we stand speechless before it. It opens a gulf that the imagination cannot clear; it opens vistas from which we instinctively shrink; it opens up abysms of time in which our whole historic period would be but a day; it opens up a world of struggle, delay, waste, failure that palls the imagination. It challenges our faith in the immanency and in the ceaseless activity of God in his world; it brings the creative energy down from its celestial abode and clothes it with the flesh and blood of animal life. It may chill and shock us; it shows us that we are of the earth earthy; yea, that we are of the animal beastly; it presses us down in matter; it puts out the lights to which we have so long turned as lighting our origin; the words "sacred," "divine," "holy," and "celestial," as applied to our origin and development, we have no longer any use for, nor for any words or ideas that set us apart from the rest of creation—above it in our origin or apart from it in our relations. The atmosphere of mystery and miracle and sanctity that our religious training has thrown around our introduction upon this planet and around our relations and destiny science dispels. Our language and many of our ideas and habits of thought date back to pre-scientific times—when there were two worlds, the heavenly and the earthly, separated by a gulf. Now we know that the two worlds are one, that they are inseparably blended; that the celestial and the terrestrial are under the same law; that we can never be any more in the heavens than we are here and now, nor any nearer the final sources of life and power; that the divine is underfoot as well as overhead; that we are part and parcel of the physical universe, and take our chances in the cosmic processes the same as the rest, and draw upon the same fund of animal life that the other creatures do. We are identified with the worm underfoot no less than with the stars overhead. We are not degraded by such a thought, but the whole of creation is lifted up. Our minds and bodies are not less divine, but all things are more divine. We have to gird up our loins and try to summon strength to see this tremendous universe as it is, alive and divine to the last particle and embosomed in the Infinite.

II

Evolution is not the final explanation of the universe, but it is probably the largest generalization of the modern mind. Science has to start somewhere, and it starts with the universe as it finds it and seeks to trace secondary or proximate causes; the evolutionist seeks to trace the footsteps of creative energy in the world of animal life. How did God make man? Out of the dust of the earth, says the Bible of our fathers. The evolutionist teaches essentially the same thing, only he does not abridge the process as the catechism has abridged it for us; he would fain unfold the whole long road that man has traveled from the first protozoic cell to the vast communities of cells that now make up his physical life. He would show how man has risen on stepping-stones of his dead self. These stepping-stones have been the animal forms below him. In them and through them something, some impulse, some force, has mounted and mounted through all the enormous lapse of geologic time. In imagination we see the dim, shadowy man, restless and struggling in a vast number of earlier forms. He has struggled upward through the invertebrates, through the fish, through the reptile, through the lower mammals, through his simian ancestors till he reaches his goal in the man we know.

Darwin was not the author of the theory of evolution, but he made the theory alive and real to the imagination. He showed us what a master key it is for unlocking the riddle of the life of the globe. He launched biological science upon a new career and made it worthy of its place in the great trilogy of sciences, astronomy, geology, and biology, of which Tennyson, in his poem "Parnassus," recognized only the first two. Had Tennyson written his poem in our day he would undoubtedly have included biology among his "terrible Muses" that tower above all others, eclipsing the glory of the great poets. Or is it true that we find it easier to accept the theory of the evolution of the worlds and suns from nebulous matter than to accept the theory of the evolution of man from the maze of the lower animal forms? It is less personal to us. The astronomer has the advantage of the biologist in one important respect: he can show us in the heavens now the process of the evolution of worlds actually going on, but the biologist cannot show us the transformation of one species into another taking place to-day. We can sound the abysses of astronomic space easier than we can sound the abysses of geologic time. The stars and the nebulae we have always with us, but where are the myriad earlier forms that were the antecedents of the present

51

animal life of the globe? True, the palaeontologist finds a more or less disjointed record of them in the stratified rocks and even in a measure the course evolution has taken, but he does not actually see it at work as does the astronomer. More than that, the forces the astronomer deals with are mechanical and chemical, but the biologist deals with a new force called life that often reverses or defies mechanical and chemical forces, but which is yet so identified and blended with them that we cannot conceive it apart from them. The stomach does not digest itself, nor gravity hold the blood in the lower extremities. The tree lifts up its weight of fluids and solids and holds aloft its fruit and foliage in spite of gravity, its growing roots split and lift the rocks; mosses and lichens disintegrate granite; vital energy triumphs over chemical and mechanical energy.

Biological laws are much more subtle and difficult to trace and formulate than chemical and mechanical laws. Hence the student of organic evolution can rarely arrive at the demonstrable certainties in this field that he can in the sphere of chemistry and mechanics. It is very doubtful if life can ever be explained in terms of these things. Life works through chemical combinations and affinities, and yet is it not more than chemistry? It works with and through mechanical principles and forces, and yet it is evidently more than mechanics. It is manifested through matter, and yet no analysis of matter can reveal its secret. It comes and goes while matter stays; we destroy life, but cannot destroy matter. It is as fugitive as the wind which fills all sails one minute and is gone the next. It avails itself of fluids and gases and the laws which govern them, but fluids and gases do not explain it. It waits upon the rains and the dews, but it is more than they are; it follows in the footsteps of the decay and disintegration of the inorganic, and yet it is not the gift of these things; it transforms the face of the earth, and yet the earth has been and will be when it was not and when it will not be. Through his knowledge and his science man performs wonders every day; he can reduce mountains to powder and seas to dry land, but he cannot create or start de novo the least throb of life. At least, he has not yet done so. With all his vast resources of mechanics and chemistry, and his insight into the mechanism of the universe, he has not yet made the least particle of inorganic matter thrill with the mysterious something we call life.

There must have been a time when life was not upon the earth and there must again come a time when it will not be. It has probably vanished from the moon and all inferior planets, and it has not yet come to the superior planets, except maybe to Mars. It must be and must have always been potential in matter, but this fact leaves the mystery as profound as ever.

Yet if the artificial production of life were to happen to-day—if in some of our laboratories living matter were produced from non-living, should we not still have to credit the event to some mysterious potency residing in matter itself? If by a lucky stroke man were to evoke the organic from the inorganic, be assured he would not evoke something from nothing, or add anything to the latent possibilities of the elements with which he works. Does not the question still remain who or what made this feat possible? One dare affirm that man cannot create life de novo any more than he can create matter. He may yet evoke life as he evokes the spark from the flint and the flame from the match or as he evokes force from the food he eats. In this latter case he does not create the force; he liberates it through the vital forces of his body. The spark from the flint and the flame from the match were called forth by a mechanical process, but the process was set going by the will which waits upon the vital process. The body with all its many functions is a complicated system of mechanical devices and chemical processes, but that which is back of all and governs all is not mechanical; the body is a machine plus something else.

The chemist or biologist who shall produce a speck of protoplasm to-day will have the credit of unlocking a power in inorganic nature; he will prove by a short cut how immanent the creative energy or the vital force of the universe is in matter. He will not have eliminated the creative energy; he will only have disclosed it and availed himself of it.

We behold spontaneous combustion, a fire self-kindled, but we do not see the activity of the particles of matter that preceded it or penetrate the secret of their mysterious affinities. The fire was potential there in the very constitution of the elements. We flout at miracles, and then we disclose an unending miracle in the life about us.

All the life upon the globe, including man with all his marvelous powers, surely originated upon the globe, surely arose out of the non-living and the non-thinking, not by the fiat of some power external to nature, but through the creative energy inherent in nature and ever active there. The great physical instrumentality was heat—without heat the reaction called life could never have taken place. This fact has led a French biologist to say that life is only a surface accident in the history of the thermic evolution of the globe. Without the disintegration of the rocks and the formation of the soil and the precipitation of watery vapor, which was indirectly the work of heat, the vegetable and the animal could not have developed. If we succeed in proving that all these things are of chemico-mechanical origin, we still want to know who or what instituted these chemical and mechanical powers and the laws that govern them.

Creation by chemistry and mechanics is as mysterious as creation by miracle. We must still have a creator, while we can do nothing with him nor find any place for him in an endless, beginningless, infinite series of events. So there we are. We go out of the same door by which we came in.

When all life vanishes from the earth, as it will when the condition of heat and moisture has radically changed, and eternal refrigeration sets in—what then? The potencies of matter will not have changed and life will reappear and go through its cycle again on some other sphere.

Life began upon this earth not by miracle in the old sense, but by miracle in the new scientific sense—by the immanence and ceaseless activity of the creative energy in the physical world about us—in the sunbeam, in the rains, in the snows, in the air currents, and in the soil underfoot; in oxygen, hydrogen, carbon, nitrogen, in lime, iron, silex, phosphorus, and in all the rest of them. Each has its laws, its ways, its fixed mode of procedure, its affinities, its likes and dislikes, and life is bound up with all of them. If we hypothesize the ether to explain certain phenomena, why should we not hypothesize a vital force to account for other mysteries?

The inorganic passes into the organic as night passes into day. Where does one end and the other begin? No man can tell. There is no beginning and no ending of either, and yet night comes and goes and day comes and goes—a constant becoming and a constant ending. We are probably in the midday of the life of the globe—life huge and rank and riotous—the youth of life has passed, life more sedate and aspiring and spiritual has come. The gigantic has gone or is going, the huge monsters of the sea and of the land have had their day, man appears at the end of the series of lesser but more complete forms.

Many intelligent persons who have been rocked in the cradle of the old creeds still look upon evolution as a godless doctrine and accuse it of vulgarizing high and sacred things. This state of mind can only be slowly outgrown by familiarizing ourselves with the processes of nature or of the creative energy in the world of life and matter about us; with our own origin in the low fishlike or apelike creature in the maternal womb; with the development of every plant, tree, and animal from a microscopic germ; with the unbroken sequence of natural law; with the waste, the delays, the pains, the failures on every hand; with the impersonal and the impartial character of all the physical forces; with the transformations and metamorphoses that marked the course of animal life; and, above all, with the thought that evolution is not self-caused or in any true sense a cause in itself, but the instrument or plan of the power that works in and through all things. The ways of God in all these details are past finding out, but science watches the unfolding of a bud, the development of a grain of wheat, the growth of the human embryo, the succession of life-forms upon the globe as revealed in the records of the stratified rocks, or observes in the heavens the condensation of nebulous matter into suns and systems, and it says this is one of his ways. Evolution—an endless unfolding and transformation. "Urge and urge and urge," says Whitman (I love to repeat this saying; it is so significant), "always the procreant urge of the world." Always the labor and travail pains of the universe to bring forth higher forms; always struggle and pain and failure and death, but always a new birth and an upward reach.

Strike out the element of time and we see evolution as the great prestidigitator of the biologic ages. The creative energy manipulates a fish and it turns into a reptile; it covers a mollusk as with a vapor and behold, a backboned creature instead! Now we see a little creature no larger than a fox and when we look again, behold the horse; a wolf or some kindred animal is plunged into the water, and behold, the seal! Some small creature of the lemur kind is covered with a capacious hand, and we look again, and behold man! We have only to minimize time and minimize space to see the impossible happening all about us or to see the Mosaic account of creation repeated; we have only the clay and water to begin with, when, presto! behold what we have now! We see the rocks covered with verdure, the mountains vanishing into plains, the valleys changing into hills or the plains changing into mountains, tropic lands covered with ice and snow.

Lord Salisbury thought he had discredited natural selection, which is one of the feet upon which evolution goes, when he charged that no one had ever seen it at work. We have not seen it at work because our little span of life is too short. Only the palaeontologist traces in the records of the rocks the footsteps of this god of change. And rarely if ever does he find a continuous and complete record—only a footprint here and there, but he sees the direction in which they are going and many of the places where the traveler tarried. The palaeontologist, that detective of the rocks, works up his case with the same thoroughness and caution and the same power of observation as does the detective in human affairs and with a greater sweep of scientific imagination.

An agent of evolution is the influence of the environment, but who sees the environment set its stamp upon animal life? After many generations we may see the accumulated results. In a few instances the results are rapid. Thus sheep lose their wool in tropical climates and a northern fur-bearing animal its fur. The well-being of the animal demands this change, and demands it quickly. Fish lose their sense of sight in underground streams; this loss is not so vital and it comes about much more slowly. A tropical climate sets its stamp upon the complexion and character of man, but this again is a slow process, as the same stress of necessity does not exist.

In the tendency to variation—in form, size, disposition, power, fertility—man differs from all other animals. In the same race, in the same family, we find infinitely varied types. Among the wild creatures all the individuals of a species are practically alike. We can hardly tell one fox, or one marmot, or one chipmunk, or one crow, or one hawk, or one black duck from another of the same species. Of course there are slight individual differences, but they are hardly distinguishable. Among the insects, one bee, one beetle, one ant, one butterfly seems the exact copy of every other individual of its kind. The law of variation seems practically annulled in the insect world.

It is the wide and free range of this law in the human species that has undoubtedly led to the great progress of the race. There has been no dead level—no democracy of talent—no equality of gifts, but only equality of opportunity. Men differ from one another in their mental endowments, capacities, and dispositions vastly more than do any other creatures upon the earth. This difference makes man's chances of progress so much the greater; he has so many more stakes in the game. If one type of talent fails, another type may win; if the lymphatic temperament is not a success, try the sanguine or the bilious; blue eyes and black eyes and brown eyes will win more triumphs than blue or black or brown alone. Arms or legs extra long, sight or hearing extra sharp, wit extra keen, judgment extra sure—all these things open doors to more progress. Variation gives natural selection a chance to take hold, and where the struggle for life is the most severe the changes will be the most rapid and the most radical. Without the pressure of the environment natural selection would not select. The tendency to physical variation in man is probably no greater than in other creatures, but his tendency to mental variation is enormous. He varies daily from mediocrity to genius, hence the enormous range of his chances of progress. From the first variation that started him on his way in his line of descent, variation must have been more and more active till he varied in the direction of reason, long before the dawn of history, since which time his progress has been by rapid strides—and more and more rapid till we see his leaps forward in recent times. The race owes its rapid progress to its exceptional men, its men of genius and power, and these have often been like sports or the sudden result of mutations—a man like Lincoln springing from the humblest parentage. No such extreme variations are seen in any of the lower orders. Indeed, in one's lifetime one sees but very slight variation in any of the wild or domestic creatures, less in the wild than in the domestic because they are less under the influence of that most variable of animals, man. And man's variations are mainly mental and not physical. The higher we go in the scale of powers, the greater the variation and hence the more rapid the evolution. Probably man's body has not changed radically in vast cycles of time, but his mind has developed enormously since the dawn of history.

IV

Biologists are coming more and more to recognize some unknown factor in evolution, probably some unknowable factor. The four factors of Osborn—heredity, ontogeny, environment, selection—play upon and modify endlessly the new form when it is started, but what about the original start? Whence comes this inborn momentum, this evolutionary send-off? What or who set the whole grand process going?

Bergson sees an internal psychological principle of development, hence the name of his book, "Creative Evolution." Osborn uses the word "directed." Certain characters, he says, are adaptive or suited to their purpose from the start; they do not have to be fitted to their place by natural selection. Huxley uses the word "predestined"—all the life of the globe and all the starry hosts of heaven are working out in boundless space and in endless time "their predestined course of evolution." Darwin must have had in mind the same mysterious something when he said that man had risen to the very summit of the animal scale, but not through his own exertions. Not by his own will or exertion, surely, any more than the embryo in its mother's womb develops into the full-grown child by its own exertion or than our temperaments and complexions and statures are matters of our own wills and choice. Something greater than man and before him, to which he sustains the relation that the unborn child sustains to its mother, must enter into our thought of his origin and development.

The great evolutionists have been very cautious about seeking to go behind evolution and name the Primal Cause. In such an attempt science would at once be beyond soundings. Darwin and Huxley were reverent, truth-loving men, but they hesitated as men of science to put themselves in a position where no step could be taken.

Slowly man emerges out of the abyss of geologic time into the dawn of history, and science gropes about like a man feeling his way in the dark or, at most, by the aid now and then of a dim flash of light, to trace the path he has come. He has surely arrived, and we are, I believe, safe in saying he has come by the way of the lower orders; but the precise forms through which he has come, the houses in which he has tarried by the way, and all the adventures and vicissitudes that befell him on the journey—can we ever hope to know these things? In any case, man has his antecedents; life has its antecedents; every beat of one's heart has its antecedent cause, which again has its antecedent. We can thus traverse the chain of causation only to find it is an endless chain; the separate links we can examine, but the first link or the last we see, by the very nature of things, and the laws of our own minds, must forever elude us. Science cannot admit of a break in the chain of causation, cannot admit that miracles or the supernatural in the old sense, as external and arbitrary interference with the natural order, can play or ever have played any part in this universe. Yet science has to postulate a First Cause when it knows, or metaphysics knows for it, that with the Infinite there can be no first and no last, no beginning and no ending, only endless succession.

To science man is not a fallen creature, but a many times risen creature and all the good of the universe centres in him. The mind that pervades all nature and is active in plant and animal alike first comes to know itself and regard itself and achieve intellectual appreciation in man. While all nature below man is wise only to its own ends and goes its appointed way as void of self-consciousness as the stone that falls or the wind that blows, the mind of man attains to disinterested wisdom and turns upon itself and upon the universe the power of objective thought; it alone achieves understanding.

In our studies of life and of the universe as soon as we begin to bridge chasms by an appeal to the miraculous, or to the extra-natural powers, we are traitors to the scientific spirit which we seek to serve. There are many things that science cannot explain. Perhaps I may say that it cannot give the ultimate explanation of anything. It can do little more than tell us of the action, the interaction, and the reaction of things, but of the things themselves, their origin and ultimate nature, or the source of the laws that govern them, what does it or what can it know?

Man is the heir of all the geologic ages; he inherits the earth after countless generations of animals and plants, and the beneficent forces of wind and rain, air and sky, have in the course of millions of years prepared it for him. His body has been built for him through the lives and struggles of the countless beings who are in the line of his long descent; his mind is equally an accumulated inheritance of the mental growth of the myriads of thinking men and unthinking animals that went before him. In the forms of his humbler forebears he has himself lived and died myriads of times to make ready the soil that nurses and sustains him to-day. He is a debtor to Cambrian and Silurian times, to the dragons and saurians and mastodons that have roamed over the earth. Indeed, what is there or has there been in the universe that he is not indebted to? The remotest star that shines has sent a ray that has entered into his life. All things are under his feet, and the keys of the heavens are in his hands.

V

One would fain arrive at some concrete belief or image of his line of descent in geologic time as he does in the historic period. But how hard it is to do so! Can we form any mental picture of the actual animal forms that the manward impulse has traveled through? With all the light that palaeontology throws upon the animal life of the past, can we see where amid the revel of these bizarre forms our ancestor hid himself? Can we see him as a reptile in the slime of the jungle or in the waters of the Mesozoic world? What was he like or what akin to? What mark or sign was there upon him at that time of the future that was before him? Can we see him as a fish in the old Devonian seas or lakes? Was he a big fish or a little fish? The primitive fishes were mostly of the shark kind. Is there any connection between that fact and the human sharks of to-day? Much less can one picture to one's self what his ancestor was like in the age of the invertebrates, amid the trilobites, etc., of the earlier Palaeozoic seas. But we must go back even earlier than that, back to unicellular life and to original protoplasm, and finally back to fiery nebulous matter. What can we make of it all by way of concrete conception of what actually took place—of the visible, eating, warring, breeding animal forms in whose safekeeping our heritage lay? Nothing. We are not merely at sea, we are in abysmal depths, and the darkness is so thick we can cut it.

We meet the same difficulty when we try to figure to ourselves the line of descent of any of the animal forms of to-day. How did they escape the world-wild catastrophe of earlier geologic times? Or did the creative impulse bank upon life as a whole and never become bankrupt, no matter what special lines or forms failed?

The first appearance of the primates is in Eocene times and the anthropoid apes in the Miocene, probably five millions of years ago. The form which may have been in our line of descent, the Dryopithecus, later appears to have become extinct. Did our fate hang upon the success of any of these forms? The monkeys and anthropoid apes appeared at the same time in different countries. Nature seems to have been making preliminary studies of man in these various forms, but when and where she hit upon the form that she perfected in man, who knows?

The horse appears to have been evolved in North America, true cattle in Asia, elephants in Africa. Can we narrow their line of descent down to a single pair for each? Many forms allied to the horse appeared in Europe and Asia in Miocene times. We find monkeys in different parts of the world in the same geologic horizons; did they all have a common origin?

Life's apprenticeship has been a long one. The earlier forms of vertebrate life were very large; later they became very small. Nature seems to have experimented with bulk, as if she thought size would win in the race. Hence those huge uncouth forms among the reptiles and early mammals. The scheme did not work well; bulk was not the thing, after all. Most of the gigantic forms became extinct. Then she tried smaller and more agile forms with larger brains—less flesh and more wit. On this line Nature continued to work till she produced her masterpiece in man—a rather feeble and nearly weaponless animal, but with an intangible armory of weapons and tools in his brain that enables him to put all creatures under his feet.

XII

THE HAZARDS OF THE PAST

I

Bergson, the new French philosopher, thinks we all had a narrow escape, back in geologic time, of having our eggs spoiled before they were hatched, or, rather, rendered incapable of hatching by too thick a shell. This was owing to the voracity of the early organisms. As they became more and more mobile, they began to take on thick armors and breastplates and shells and calcareous skins to protect themselves from one another. This tendency resulted, he thinks, in the arrest of the entire animal world in its evolution toward higher and higher forms. These shells and armors begat a kind of torpor and immobility which has continued down to our day with the echinoderms and mollusks, but the arthropods and vertebrates escaped it by some lucky stroke. Now you and I are here without imprisoning shells on our backs; but how or why did we escape? Bergson does not say. Was it a matter of luck or chance? Was there ever a time when the stream of life tended to harden and become fixed in its own forms like a stream of cooling lava, or has the innate plasticity of life been easily equal to its own ends? True, the clam remains a clam, and the starfish remains a starfish; some other forms have carried the evolutionary impulse forward till it flowered in man. Was this impulse ever really checked or endangered? Was the golden secret ever intrusted to the keeping of any single form? and, had that form been cut off, would the earth have been still without its man? These are puzzling questions.

Thus, when we have come to look upon life and nature in the light of evolution, what vistas are opened to us where before were only blank walls! The geologic ages take on a new interest to us. We know that in some form we were even there. The systems of sedimentary rocks which the geologist portrays, piled one upon the other to a depth of fifty miles or more, seem like the stairway by which we have ascended, taking on some new and more developed form at each rise. What we were at the first step in Cambrian times only the Lord knows, but whatever we were, we crept up or floated up to the next rise. In the Silurian seas we may have been a trilobite for aught we know; at any rate, we were the outcome of the life impulse that begat the trilobites, but our fate was not bound up with theirs, as their race came to an end in those early geologic ages, and our stem form did not. Whether or not we were a fish in the Devonian seas, there is little doubt that we had gills, because we have the gill slits yet in our early foetal life, and it is quite certain that in some way we owe our backbones to the fishes.

When the rocks that form my native Catskills were being laid down in the Devonian waters, I fancy that my aquatic embryo was swimming about somewhere and slowly waxing strong. Up and up I climbed across the sandstone steps, across the limestone, the conglomerate, the slate, up into Carboniferous times. The upper and nether millstones of the "millstone grit" did not crush me, neither did the floods and the convulsions of Carboniferous times that buried the vast vegetable growths that resulted in our coal measures engulf or destroy me. About that time probably, I emerged from the water and became an amphibian, and maybe got my five fingers and five toes on each side.

Nor did the wholesale destruction of animal life at the end of Palaeozoic time cut off my line of descent. The monstrous reptiles of the succeeding or Mesozoic age, the petrified remains of one of which was recently found in the sandstone rocks near the river's edge under the Palisades of the Hudson, do not seem to have endangered the golden thread by which our fate hung. Still "I mount and mount." The stairs by which I climb were rent by earthquakes and volcanoes, the strata were squeezed up and overturned and folded in the great mountain-chains; the Alps, the Andes, the Himalayas, the Coast Range were born; the earth-throes must have been tremendous at times; yet I escaped it all. The huge and fearful mammals of the third or Tertiary period passed me by unharmed. Eruptions and cataclysms, the sinking of the land, the inundations of the sea, world-wide deformations of the earth's crust, fire and ice and floods, monsters of the deep and dragons of the land and the air have beset my course from the first, and yet here I am, here we all are, and apparently none the worse for the appalling dangers we have passed through.

56

Evolution thus makes the world over for us. It shows us in what a complex web of vital and far-reaching relations we stand. It gives us an outlook upon the past that is startling, and in some ways forbidding, yet one that ought to be stimulating and inspiring. If we look back with a shudder we should look forward with a thrill. If the past is terrible, the future is in the same degree cheering and inviting. If we came out of those lowly and groveling forms, to what heights of being may we not be carried by the impetus that brought us thus far? In fact, to what heights has it already carried us!

II

That the hazards of the past, to many forms of life, at least, have been real and no myth, is evident from the vast number of forms that have been cut off and become extinct; various causes, now hard to decipher, have worked together to the end, such as changed geographical conditions, changes of climate, affecting the food-supply, extreme specialization, like that of the sabre-toothed tiger whose petrified remains have been found in various parts of this continent, and who apparently was finally handicapped by his huge dental sabre. Probably many more species of animals have become extinct than have survived, but none of these could have been in the line of man's descent, else the human race would not have been here. If the Eocene progenitor of the horse, the little four-toed eohippus, had been cut off, would not the world have been horseless to-day? The horse in America became extinct, from some cause only conjectural, many tens of thousands of years ago. Had the same fate befallen the horse in Europe and Asia, it seems probable that our civilization would have been far less advanced to-day than it is.

The fate of every species of mammal in our time seems to have been in the keeping of a single form in early Tertiary times. The end of the Cretaceous or chalk period saw the extinction of the giant reptiles both of sea and of land, at the same time that it saw the appearance of a great many species of small and inconspicuous mammals, among which doubtless were our own humble forebears. Extreme specialization in any direction may narrow an animal's chances of survival; they have but one chance in the game of life, whereas an animal with a more generalized organization has many chances. Man is one of the most generalized of animals; no special tools, no special weapons—his hand many tools and weapons in one. Hence he is the most adaptable of animals; all climes, all foods, all places are his; he is master of the land, of the sea, of the air.

Animal life is often curiously interdependent. I asked our guide in the Adirondacks if there were any ravens there. "Not nearly as many as there used to be," he said, and his explanation of their disappearance seems thoroughly scientific; it was that the wolves and the panthers kept them in meat, and now that these animals had disappeared, the ravens had little to feed upon. If the moose were compelled to graze from off the ground, like a sheep or a cow, the species would probably soon become extinct. Osborn thinks it probable that the huge beast called titanothere finally became extinct early in Tertiary times owing to the form of its teeth, which were of such a type that they could not change to meet a change in the flora upon which the creature fed. Of course we shall never know what narrow escapes our race had from extinction in the remote past; some forms have ended in a blind alley, like the sea-urchin and the oyster. Arthropoda have continued to evolve and have reached their high-water mark of intelligence in bees and ants. The vertebrates went forward and have culminated in man. Bergson thinks that in the vertebrates intelligence has been developed at the expense of instinct, and that in the invertebrates instinct has been perfected at the expense of intelligence.

Are we not compelled to adopt what is called the monophyletic hypothesis, that is, that our line of descent started from one pair, male and female, somewhere in the vast stretch of geologic or biologic time, and to reason that, had that pair been out of the race, we should not have appeared?

Can we narrow life to a single point, a single cell, in the past? Was there one and only one first bit of protoplasm? If we were to say that life first appeared on the globe in Cambrian times, just what should we mean? That it began as a single point, or as many points? When we say that the primates first appeared in Eocene times, do we mean that one single primate appeared then? If so, what form went immediately before him? This is all a vain speculation.

Does man presuppose all the vertebrate sub-kingdom? Was he safe as long as one vertebrate form remained? Are his forebears many, and not one pair? Can we think of his ancestry under the image of a tree, and of him as one of the many branches? If so, nothing but the destruction of the tree would have imperiled his appearance, or the lopping off of his particular branch. Probably all such images are misleading. We simply cannot figure to ourselves the tangled course of our biological descent. If thwartings and accidents and delays could have cut man off, how could he have escaped? We cannot think of man as one; we are compelled to think of him as many; and yet in all our experience the many come from the one, or the one pair.

How thick the field of animal life in the past is strewn with extinct forms!—as thick as the sidereal spaces are strewn with the fragments of wrecked worlds! But other worlds and suns are spun out of the wrecked worlds and suns through the process of cosmic evolution. The world-stuff is worked over and over. Extinct animal forms must have given rise to other, allied forms before they perished, and these to still others, and so on down to our time.

The image of a tree is misleading from the fact that all the different branches of the animal kingdom, from the protozoa up to man, have come along with what we call the higher branches, the mammals; the suckers have kept pace with the main stalk, so that we have the image of a sheaf of branches starting from a common origin and all of equal length. Man has brought on his relations along with him.

There is no glamour of romance over that past. It was all hard, prosy, terrible fact. The earth's crust was less stable than now, the upheavals and subsidences and earthquakes more frequent, the warring of the elements more fierce and incessant, deluge and inundation in more rapid succession, and the riot and excesses of animal life far beyond anything we know of. And our line of descent was taking its chances amid it all. The widespread blotting out of life at the end of Palaeozoic time, and again at the end of Mesozoic times, when myriads of forms were cut off, probably from some convulsion of nature or some cosmic catastrophe; and again during the ice age, when the camel, the llama, the horse, the tapir, the mastodon, the elephant, the giant sloth, became extinct in North America—how fared it with our ancestor during these terrible ages? There is no sure trace of him till late Tertiary times, and it is probably not more than two hundred thousand years ago that he assumed the upright attitude and began to use tools. Probably in Europe fifty thousand years ago he was living in caves, clothed in skins, contending with the cave bear and cave lion, using rude stone implements, and hunting the hairy mastodon, etc. In Asia the probabilities are that he was farther on the road toward the dawn of history.

We may think of our descent in the historic period under the image of the stream, though of a stream many times delayed and diverted, even many times diminished by wars and plagues and famine, but a stream with some sort of unity and continuity, since man became man. The stream of life is like any other stream in this respect. Divert or use up part of the water of a stream, yet what is left flows on and keeps up the continuity and identity of the stream; dip your cup into it here, and you will not get precisely the same water you would have got had none of it been diverted or used far back in its course—you get the water that was allowed to flow by.

Had there been no loss of life by war and pestilence and accidents of various kinds, the different countries would have been occupied by quite other men and women than those that fill them to-day. The course of life in every neighborhood is changed by what seem like accidental causes, as when a family is practically wiped out by some accident or dread disease. This brings new people on the scene. The farm or the business falls into other hands, and new social relations spring up, new men and women are brought together or the old ones driven apart, marriage is hastened or retarded, opportunities for family life are made or unmade, and fewer children, or more children, as the case may be, are the result. The issue of some battle hundreds or thousands of years ago may have played a part in your life and mine to-day—other races, other individuals of the race, would have been thrown together had the issue been different, and other families started, so that some one else would have been here in our stead.

But the question of hazard to the race of man in geologic time is quite a different one. Here our fate seems to hang by a single thread—a golden thread, we may call it, but, in that terrible maze of clashing forces and devouring forms of the vast geologic periods, how liable to be broken! It is not now a question of the continuity of a stream, but of the continuity of a single evolutionary process, or, as Haeckel says, the continuity of the morphological chain which stretches from the lemurs up through tailed and tailless anthropoid apes to man. If the evolutionary impulse had been checked or extinguished in the lemur—that small apelike animal that went before the true ape, the fossil remains of which have been found on this continent and the survivals of which are now found in Madagascar—would man have appeared? Again, if the race of lemurs developed from a single pair, how precarious seems our fate! In fact, if any of the transitional forms between species can be reduced to a single pair—as the forms that connect the reptiles with the mammals—our fate would seem to be in the keeping of these forms. Over this single frail bridge which escaped the floods and the tornadoes and the earthquakes of those terrible ages we must have passed. What risky business it all seems! Was it luck or law that favored us? Doubtless, if we could penetrate the mystery, we should see that there was no chance or risk in the matter. We cannot go very far in solving these great fundamental questions by applying to them the tests of our own experience, Numberless specific forms become extinct, but the impulse that begat the form does not die out. Thus, all the giant reptiles died out—the dinosaurs, the mesosaurs—but the reptilian impulse still survives. How many types of invertebrates have perished! but the invertebrate impulse still goes on. How many species of mammals have been cut off! yet the mammal impulse has steadily gone forward. These things suggest the wave that moves on but leaves the water behind. The vertebrate impulse began in

58

wormlike forms, in the old Palaeozoic seas, and stopped not till it culminated in man. This impulse has left many forms behind it; but has this impulse itself ever been endangered? If one looks at the matter thus in an abstract instead of a concrete way, the problem of our descent becomes easier.

When we look at the evolution of life on a grand scale, nature seems to feel her way, like a blind man, groping, hesitating, trying this road and then that. In some cases the line of evolution seems to end in a cul de sac beyond which no progress is possible. The forms thus cornered soon become extinct. The mystery, the unaccountable thing, is the appearance of new characters. The slow modification or transformation of an existing character may often be traced; natural selection, or the struggle for existence, takes it in hand and adapts and perpetuates it, or else eliminates it. But the origin of certain new parts or characters—that is the secret of the evolutionary process. Thus there was a time when no animal had horns; then horns appeared. "In the great quadruped known as titanothere," says Osborn, "rudiments of horns first arise independently at certain definite parts of the skull; they arise at first alike in both sexes, or asexually; then they become sexual, or chiefly characteristic of males; then they rapidly evolve in the males while being arrested in development in the females; finally, they become in some of the animals dominant characteristics to which all others bend." Nature seems to throw out these new characters and then lets them take their chances in the clash of forces and tendencies that go on in the arena of life. If they serve a purpose or are an advantage, they remain; if not, they drop out. Nature feels her way. The horns proved of less advantage to the females than to the males; they seem a part of the plus or overflow of the male principle, like the beard in man—the badge of masculinity. The titanothere is traceable back to a hornless animal the size of a sheep, and it ended in a horned quadruped nearly as large as an elephant. It flourished in Wyoming in early Tertiary times. Nature did not seem to know what to do with horns when she first got them. She played with them like a child with a new toy. Thus she gave two pairs to several species of mammals, one pair on the nose and one pair on the top of the skull—certainly an embarrassment of weapons.

The first horns appear to have been crude, heavy, uncouth, but long before we reach our own geologic era they appear in various species of quadrupeds, and become graceful and ornamental. How beautiful they are in many of the African antelope tribe! Nature's workmanship nearly always improves with time, like that of man's, and sooner or later takes on an ornamental phase.

The early uncouth, bizarre forms seem to be the result of the excess or surplus of life. Life in remote biologic times was rank and riotous, as it is now, in a measure, in tropical lands. One reason may be that the climate of the globe during the middle period, and well into the third period, appears to have been of a tropical character. The climatic and seasonal divisions were not at all pronounced, and both animal and vegetable life took on gigantic and grotesque forms. In the ugliness of alligator and rhinoceros and hippopotamus of our day we get some hint of what early reptilian and mammalian life was like.

That Nature should have turned out better and better handiwork as the ages passed; that she either should have improved upon every model or else discarded it; that she should have progressed from the bird, half-dragon, to the sweet songsters of our day and to the superb forms of the air that we know; that evolution should have entered upon a refining and spiritualizing phase, developing larger brains and smaller bodies, is a very significant fact, and one quite beyond the range of the mechanistic conception of life.

Our own immediate line of descent leads down through the minor forms of Tertiary and Mesozoic times—forms that probably skulked and dodged about amid the terrible and gigantic creatures of those ages as the small game of to-day hide and flee from the presence of their arch-enemy, man; and that the frail line upon which the fate of the human race hung should not have been severed during the wild turmoil of those ages is, to me, a source of perpetual wonder.

III

The hazards of the future of the race must be quite different from those I have been considering. They are the hazards incident to an exceptional being upon this earth—a being that takes his fate in his own hands in a sense that no other creature does.

Man has partaken of the fruit of the Tree of Good and Evil, which all the lower orders have escaped. He knows, and knows that he knows. Will this knowledge, through the opposition in which it places him to elemental nature and the vast system of artificial things with which it has enabled him to surround himself, cut short his history upon this planet? Will Nature in the end be avenged for the secrets he has forced from her? His civilization has doubtless made him the victim of diseases to which the lower orders, and even savage man, are strangers. Will not these diseases increase as his life becomes more and more complex and artificial? Will he go on extending his mastery over Nature and refining or suppressing his natural appetites till his original hold upon life is fatally enfeebled?

It seems as though science ought to save man and prolong his stay on this planet,—it ought to bring him natural salvation, as his religion promises him supernatural salvation. But of course, man's fate is bound up with the fate of the planet and of the biological tree of which he is one of the shoots. Biology is rooted in geology. The higher forms of life did not arbitrarily appear, they flowed out of conditions that were long in maturing; they flowered in season, and the flower will fall in season. Man could not have appeared earlier than he did, nor later than he did; he came out of what went before, and he will go out with what comes after. His coming was natural, and his going will be natural. His period had a beginning, and it will have an end. Natural philosophy leads one to affirm this; but of time measured by human history he may yet have a lease of tens of thousands of years.

The hazard of the future is a question of both astronomy and geology. That there are cosmic dangers, though infinitely remote, every astronomer knows. That there are collisions between heavenly bodies is an indubitable fact, and if collisions do happen to any, allow time enough and they must happen to all. That there are geologic dangers through the shifting and crumpling of the earth's crust, every geologist knows, though probably none that could wipe out the whole race of man. The biologic dangers of the past we have outlived—the dangers that must have beset a single line of descent amid the carnival of power and the ferocity of the monster reptiles of Mesozoic times, and the wholesale extinction of species that occurred in different geologic periods.

Nothing but a cosmic catastrophe, involving the fate of the whole earth, could now exterminate the human race. It is highly improbable that this will ever happen. The race of man will go out from a slow, insensible failure, through the aging of the planet, of the conditions of life that brought man here. The evolutionary process upon a cooling world must, after the elapse of a vast period of time, lose its impetus and cease.

XIII

THE GOSPEL OF NATURE

I

The other day a clergyman who described himself as a preacher of the gospel of Christ wrote, asking me to come and talk to his people on the gospel of Nature. The request set me to thinking whether or not Nature has any gospel in the sense the clergyman had in mind, any message that is likely to be specially comforting to the average orthodox religious person. I suppose the parson wished me to tell his flock what I had found in Nature that was a strength or a solace to myself.

What had all my many years of journeyings to Nature yielded me that would supplement or reinforce the gospel he was preaching? Had the birds taught me any valuable lessons? Had the four-footed beasts? Had the insects? Had the flowers, the trees, the soil, the coming and the going of the seasons? Had I really found sermons in stones, books in running brooks and good in everything? Had the lilies of the field, that neither toil nor spin, and yet are more royally clad than Solomon in all his glory, helped me in any way to clothe myself with humility, with justice, with truthfulness?

It is not easy for one to say just what he owes to all these things. Natural influences work indirectly as well as directly; they work upon the subconscious, as well as upon the conscious, self. That I am a saner, healthier, more contented man, with truer standards of life, for all my loiterings in the fields and woods, I am fully convinced.

That I am less social, less interested in my neighbors and in the body politic, more inclined to shirk civic and social responsibilities and to stop my ears against the brawling of the reformers, is perhaps equally true.

One thing is certain, in a hygienic way I owe much to my excursions to Nature. They have helped to clothe me with health, if not with humility; they have helped sharpen and attune all my senses; they have kept my eyes in such good trim that they have not failed me for one moment during all the seventy-five years I have had them; they have made my sense of smell so keen that I have much pleasure in the wild, open-air perfumes, especially in the spring—the delicate breath of the blooming elms and maples and willows, the breath of the woods, of the pastures, of the shore. This keen, healthy sense of smell has made me abhor tobacco and flee from close rooms, and put the stench of cities behind me. I fancy that this whole world of wild, natural perfumes is lost to the tobacco-user and to the city-dweller. Senses trained in the open air are in tune with open-air objects; they are quick, delicate, and discriminating. When I go to town, my ear suffers as well as my nose: the impact of the city upon my senses is hard and dissonant; the ear is stunned, the nose is outraged, and the eye is confused. When I come back, I go to Nature to be soothed and healed, and to have my senses put in tune once more. I know that, as a rule, country or farming folk are not remarkable for the delicacy of their senses, but this is owing mainly to the benumbing and brutalizing effect of continued hard labor. It is their minds more than their bodies that suffer.

When I have dwelt in cities the country was always near by, and I used to get a bite of country soil at least once a week to keep my system normal.

Emerson says that "the day does not seem wholly profane in which we have given heed to some natural object." If Emerson had stopped to qualify his remark, he would have added, if we give heed to it in the right spirit, if we give heed to it as a nature-lover and truth-seeker. Nature love as Emerson knew it, and as Wordsworth knew it, and as any of the choicer spirits of our time have known it, has distinctly a religious value. It does not come to a man or a woman who is wholly absorbed in selfish or worldly or material ends. Except ye become in a measure as little children, ye cannot enter the kingdom of Nature— as Audubon entered it, as Thoreau entered it, as Bryant and Amiel entered it, and as all those enter it who make it a resource in their lives and an instrument of their culture. The forms and creeds of religion change, but the sentiment of religion—the wonder and reverence and love we feel in the presence of the inscrutable universe—persists. Indeed, these seem to be renewing their life to-day in this growing love for all natural objects and in this increasing tenderness toward all forms of life. If we do not go to church so much as did our fathers, we go to the woods much more, and are much more inclined to make a temple of them than they were.

We now use the word Nature very much as our fathers used the word God, and, I suppose, back of it all we mean the power that is everywhere present and active, and in whose lap the visible universe is held and nourished. It is a power that we can see and touch and hear, and realize every moment of our lives how absolutely we are dependent upon it. There are no atheists or skeptics in regard to this power. All men see how literally we are its children, and all men learn how swift and sure is the penalty of disobedience to its commands.

Our associations with Nature vulgarize it and rob it of its divinity. When we come to see that the celestial and the terrestrial are one, that time and eternity are one, that mind and matter are one, that death and life are one, that there is and can be nothing not inherent in Nature, then we no longer look for or expect a far-off, unknown God.

Nature teaches more than she preaches. There are no sermons in stones. It is easier to get a spark out of a stone than a moral. Even when it contains a fossil, it teaches history rather than morals. It comes down from the fore-world an undigested bit that has resisted the tooth and maw of time, and can tell you many things if you have the eye to read them. The soil upon which it lies or in which it is imbedded was rock, too, back in geologic time, but the mill that ground it up passed the fragment of stone through without entirely reducing it. Very likely it is made up of the minute remains of innumerable tiny creatures that lived and died in the ancient seas. Very likely it was torn from its parent rock and brought to the place where it now lies by the great ice-flood that many tens of thousands of years ago crept slowly but irresistibly down out of the North over the greater part of all the northern continents.

But all this appeals to the intellect, and contains no lesson for the moral nature. If we are to find sermons in stones, we are to look for them in the relations of the stones to other things—when they are out of place, when they press down the grass or the flowers, or impede the plow, or dull the scythe, or usurp the soil, or shelter vermin, as do old institutions and old usages that have had their day. A stone that is much knocked about gets its sharp angles worn off, as do men. "A rolling stone gathers no moss," which is not bad for the stone, as moss hastens decay. "Killing two birds with one stone" is a bad saying, because it reminds boys to stone the birds, which is bad for both boys and birds. But "People who live in glass houses should not throw stones" is on the right side of the account, as it discourages stone-throwing and reminds us that we are no better than our neighbors.

The lesson in running brooks is that motion is a great purifier and health-producer. When the brook ceases to run, it soon stagnates. It keeps in touch with the great vital currents when it is in motion, and unites with other brooks to help make the river. In motion it soon leaves all mud and sediment behind. Do not proper work and the exercise of will power have the same effect upon our lives?

The other day in my walk I came upon a sap-bucket that had been left standing by the maple tree all the spring and summer. What a bucketful of corruption was that, a mixture of sap and rainwater that had rotted, and smelled to heaven. Mice and birds and insects had been drowned in it, and added to its unsavory character. It was a bit of Nature cut off from the vitalizing and purifying chem- istry of the whole. With what satisfaction I emptied it upon the ground while I held my nose and saw it filter into the turf, where I knew it was dying to go and where I knew every particle of the reeking, fetid fluid would soon be made sweet and wholesome again by the chemistry of the soil!

II

I am not always in sympathy with nature-study as pursued in the schools, as if this kingdom could be carried by assault. Such study is too cold, too special, too mechanical; it is likely to rub the bloom off

Nature. It lacks soul and emotion; it misses the accessories of the open air and its exhilarations, the sky, the clouds, the landscape, and the currents of life that pulse everywhere.

I myself have never made a dead set at studying Nature with note-book and field-glass in hand. I have rather visited with her. We have walked together or sat down together, and our intimacy grows with the seasons. What I have learned about her ways I have learned easily, almost unconsciously, while fishing or camping or idling about. My desultory habits have their disadvantages, no doubt, but they have their advantages also. A too strenuous pursuit defeats itself. In the fields and woods more than anywhere else all things come to those who wait, because all things are on the move, and are sure sooner or later to come your way.

To absorb a thing is better than to learn it, and we absorb what we enjoy. We learn things at school, we absorb them in the fields and woods and on the farm. When we look upon Nature with fondness and appreciation she meets us halfway and takes a deeper hold upon us than when studiously conned. Hence I say the way of knowledge of Nature is the way of love and enjoyment, and is more surely found in the open air than in the school-room or the laboratory. The other day I saw a lot of college girls dissecting cats and making diagrams of the circulation and muscle-attachments, and I thought it pretty poor business unless the girls were taking a course in comparative anatomy with a view to some occupation in life. What is the moral and intellectual value of this kind of knowledge to those girls? Biology is, no doubt, a great science in the hands of great men, but it is not for all. I myself have got along very well without it. I am sure I can learn more of what I want to know from a kitten on my knee than from the carcass of a cat in the laboratory. Darwin spent eight years dissecting barnacles; but he was Darwin, and did not stop at barnacles, as these college girls are pretty sure to stop at cats. He dissected and put together again in his mental laboratory the whole system of animal life, and the upshot of his work was a tremendous gain to our understanding of the universe.

I would rather see the girls in the fields and woods studying and enjoying living nature, training their eyes to see correctly and their hearts to respond intelligently. What is knowledge without enjoyment, without love? It is sympathy, appreciation, emotional experience, which refine and elevate and breathe into exact knowledge the breath of life. My own interest is in living nature as it moves and flourishes about me winter and summer.

I know it is one thing to go forth as a nature-lover, and quite another to go forth in a spirit of cold, calculating, exact science. I call myself a nature-lover and not a scientific naturalist. All that science has to tell me is welcome, is, indeed, eagerly sought for. I must know as well as feel. I am not merely contented, like Wordsworth's poet, to enjoy what others understand. I must understand also; but above all things I must enjoy. How much of my enjoyment springs from my knowledge I do not know. The joy of knowing is very great; the delight of picking up the threads of meaning here and there, and following them through the maze of confusing facts, I know well. When I hear the woodpecker drumming on a dry limb in spring or the grouse drumming in the woods, and know what it is all for, why, that knowledge, I suppose, is part of my enjoyment. The other part is the associations that those sounds call up as voicing the arrival of spring: they are the drums that lead the joyous procession.

To enjoy understandingly, that, I fancy, is the great thing to be desired. When I see the large ichneumon-fly, Thalessa, making a loop over her back with her long ovipositor and drilling a hole in the trunk of a tree, I do not fully appreciate the spectacle till I know she is feeling for the burrow of a tree-borer, Tremex, upon the larvae of which her own young feed. She must survey her territory like an oil-digger and calculate where she is likely to strike oil, which in her case is the burrow of her host Tremex. There is a vast series of facts in natural history like this that are of little interest until we understand them. They are like the outside of a book which may attract us, but which can mean little to us until we have opened and perused its pages.

The nature-lover is not looking for mere facts, but for meanings, for something he can translate into the terms of his own life. He wants facts, but significant facts—luminous facts that throw light upon the ways of animate and inanimate nature. A bird picking up crumbs from my window-sill does not mean much to me. It is a pleasing sight and touches a tender cord, but it does not add much to my knowledge of bird-life. But when I see a bird pecking and fluttering angrily at my window-pane, as I now and then do in spring, apparently under violent pressure to get in, I am witnessing a significant comedy in bird-life, one that illustrates the limits of animal instinct. The bird takes its own reflected image in the glass for a hated rival, and is bent on demolishing it. Let the assaulting bird get a glimpse of the inside of the empty room through a broken pane, and it is none the wiser; it returns to the assault as vigorously as ever.

The fossils in the rocks did not mean much to the earlier geologists. They looked upon them as freaks of Nature, whims of the creative energy, or vestiges of Noah's flood. You see they were blinded by the preconceived notions of the six-day theory of creation.

III

I do not know that the bird has taught me any valuable lesson. Indeed, I do not go to Nature to be taught. I go for enjoyment and companionship. I go to bathe in her as in a sea; I go to give my eyes and ears and all my senses a free, clean field and to tone up my spirits by her "primal sanities." If the bird has not preached to me, it has added to the resources of my life, it has widened the field of my interests, it has afforded me another beautiful object to love, and has helped make me feel more at home in this world. To take the birds out of my life would be like lopping off so many branches from the tree: there is so much less surface of leafage to absorb the sunlight and bring my spirits in contact with the vital currents. We cannot pursue any natural study with love and enthusiasm without the object of it becoming a part of our lives. The birds, the flowers, the trees, the rocks, all become linked with our lives and hold the key to our thoughts and emotions.

Not till the bird becomes a part of your life can its coming and its going mean much to you. And it becomes a part of your life when you have taken heed of it with interest and affection, when you have established associations with it, when it voices the spring or the summer to you, when it calls up the spirit of the woods or the fields or the shore. When year after year you have heard the veery in the beech and birch woods along the trout streams, or the wood thrush May after May in the groves where you have walked or sat, and the bobolink summer after summer in the home meadows, or the vesper sparrow in the upland pastures where you have loitered as a boy or mused as a man, these birds will really be woven into the texture of your life.

What lessons the birds have taught me I cannot recall; what a joy they have been to me I know well. In a new place, amid strange scenes, theirs are the voices and the faces of old friends. In Bermuda the bluebirds and the catbirds and the cardinals seemed to make American territory of it. Our birds had annexed the island despite the Britishers.

For many years I have in late April seen the red-poll warbler, perhaps for only a single day, flitting about as I walked or worked. It is usually my first warbler, and my associations with it are very pleasing. But I really did not know how pleasing until, one March day, when I was convalescing from a serious illness in one of our sea-coast towns, I chanced to spy the little traveler in a vacant lot along the street, now upon the ground, now upon a bush, nervous and hurried as usual, uttering its sharp chip, and showing the white in its tail. The sight gave me a real home feeling. It did me more good than the medicine I was taking. It instantly made a living link with many past springs. Anything that calls up a happy past, how it warms the present! There, too, that same day I saw my first meadowlark of the season in a vacant lot, flashing out the white quills in her tail, and walking over the turf in the old, erect, alert manner. The sight was as good as a letter from home, and better: it had a flavor of the wild and of my boyhood days on the old farm that no letter could ever have.

The spring birds always awaken a thrill wherever I am. The first bobolink I hear flying over northward and bursting out in song now and then, full of anticipation of those broad meadows where he will soon be with his mate; or the first swallow twittering joyously overhead, borne on a warm southern breeze; or the first high-hole sounding out his long, iterated call from the orchard or field—how all these things send a wave of emotion over me!

Pleasures of another kind are to find a new bird, and to see an old bird in a new place, as I did recently in the old sugar-bush where I used to help gather and boil sap as a boy. It was the logcock, or pileated woodpecker, a rare bird anywhere, and one I had never seen before on the old farm. I heard his loud cackle in a maple tree, saw him flit from branch to branch for a few moments, and then launch out and fly toward a distant wood. But he left an impression with me that I should be sorry to have missed.

Nature stimulates our aesthetic and our intellectual life and to a certain extent our religious emotions, but I fear we cannot find much support for our ethical system in the ways of wild Nature. I know our artist naturalist, Ernest Thompson Seton, claims to find what we may call the biological value of the Ten Commandments in the lives of the wild animals; but I cannot make his reasoning hold water, at least not much of it. Of course the Ten Commandments are not arbitrary laws. They are largely founded upon the needs of the social organism; but whether they have the same foundation in the needs of animal life apart from man, apart from the world of moral obligation, is another question. The animals are neither moral nor immoral: they are unmoral; their needs are all physical. It is true that the command against murder is pretty well kept by the higher animals. They rarely kill their own kind: hawks do not prey upon hawks, nor foxes prey upon foxes, nor weasels upon weasels; but lower down this does not hold. Trout eat trout, and pickerel eat pickerel, and among the insects young spiders eat one another, and the female spider eats her mate, if she can get him. There is but little, if any, neighborly love among even the higher animals. They treat one another as rivals, or associate for mutual protection. One cow will lick and comb another in the most affectionate manner, and the next moment savagely gore her. Hate and

63

cruelty for the most part rule in the animal world. A few of the higher animals are monogamous, but by far the greater number of species are polygamous or promiscuous. There is no mating or pairing in the great bovine tribe, and none among the rodents that I know of, or among the bear family, or the cat family, or among the seals. When we come to the birds, we find mating, and occasional pairing for life, as with the ostrich and perhaps the eagle.

As for the rights of property among the animals, I do not see how we can know just how far those rights are respected among individuals of the same species. We know that bees will rob bees, and that ants will rob ants; but whether or not one chipmunk or one flying squirrel or one wood mouse will plunder the stores of another I do not know. Probably not, as the owner of such stores is usually on hand to protect them. Moreover, these provident little creatures all lay up stores in the autumn, before the season of scarcity sets in, and so have no need to plunder one another. In case the stores of one squirrel were destroyed by some means, and it were able to dispossess another of its hoard, would it not in that case be a survival of the fittest, and so conducive to the well-being of the race of squirrels?

I have never known any of our wild birds to steal the nesting-material of another bird of the same kind, but I have known birds to try to carry off the material belonging to other species.

But usually the rule of might is the rule of right among the animals. As to most of the other commandments,—of coveting, of bearing false witness, of honoring the father and the mother, and so forth,—how can these apply to the animals or have any biological value to them? Parental obedience among them is not a very definite thing. There is neither obedience nor disobedience, because there are no commands. The alarm-cries of the parents are quickly understood by the young, and their actions imitated in the presence of danger, all of which of course has a biological value.

The instances which Mr. Seton cites of animals fleeing to man for protection from their enemies prove to my mind only how the greater fear drives out the lesser. The hotly pursued animal sees a possible cover in a group of men and horses or in an unoccupied house, and rushes there to hide. What else could the act mean? So a hunted deer or sheep will leap from a precipice which, under ordinary circumstances, it would avoid. So would a man. Fear makes bold in such cases.

I certainly have found "good in everything,"—in all natural processes and products,—not the "good" of the Sunday-school books, but the good of natural law and order, the good of that system of things out of which we came and which is the source of our health and strength. It is good that fire should burn, even if it consumes your house; it is good that force should crush, even if it crushes you; it is good that rain should fall, even if it destroys your crops or floods your land. Plagues and pestilences attest the constancy of natural law. They set us to cleaning our streets and houses and to readjusting our relations to outward nature. Only in a live universe could disease and death prevail. Death is a phase of life, a redistributing of the type. Decay is another kind of growth.

Yes, good in everything, because law in everything, truth in everything, the sequence of cause and effect in everything, and it may all be good to me if on the right principles I relate my life to it. I can make the heat and the cold serve me, the winds and the floods, gravity and all the chemical and dynamical forces, serve me, if I take hold of them by the right handle. The bad in things arises from our abuse or misuse of them or from our wrong relations to them. A thing is good or bad according as it stands related to my constitution. We say the order of nature is rational; but is it not because our reason is the outcome of that order? Our well-being consists in learning it and in adjusting our lives to it. When we cross it or seek to contravene it, we are destroyed. But Nature in her universal procedures is not rational, as I am rational when I weed my garden, prune my trees, select my seed or my stock, or arm myself with tools or weapons. In such matters I take a short cut to that which Nature reaches by a slow, roundabout, and wasteful process. How does she weed her garden? By the survival of the fittest. How does she select her breeding-stock? By the law of battle; the strongest rules. Hers, I repeat, is a slow and wasteful process. She fertilizes the soil by plowing in the crop. She cannot take a short cut. She assorts and arranges her goods by the law of the winds and the tides. She builds up with one hand and pulls down with the other. Man changes the conditions to suit the things. Nature changes the things to suit the conditions. She adapts the plant or the animal to its environment. She does not drain her marshes; she fills them up. Hers is the larger reason—the reason of the All. Man's reason introduces a new method; it cuts across, modifies, or abridges the order of Nature. I do not see design in Nature in the old ideological sense; but I see everything working to its own proper end, and that end is foretold in the means. Things are not designed; things are begotten. It is as if the final plan of a man's house, after he had begun to build it, should be determined by the winds and the rains and the shape of the ground upon which it stands. The eye is begotten by those vibrations in the ether called light, the ear by those vibrations in the air called sound, the sense of smell by those emanations called odors. There are probably other vibrations and emanations that we have no senses for because our well-being does not demand them.

We think it reasonable that a stone should fall and that smoke should rise because we have never known either of them to do the contrary. We think it reasonable that fire should burn and that frost should freeze, because this accords with universal experience. Thus, there is a large order of facts that are reasonable because they are invariable: the same effect always follows the same cause. Our reason is developed and disciplined by observing the order of Nature; and yet human rationality is of another order from the rationality of Nature. Man learns from Nature how to master and control her. He turns her currents into new channels; he spurs her in directions of his own. Nature has no economic or scientific rationality. She progresses by the method of trial and error. Her advance is symbolized by that of the child learning to walk. She experiments endlessly. Evolution has worked all around the horizon. In feeling her way to man she has produced thousands of other forms of life. The globe is peopled as it is because the creative energy was blind and did not at once find the single straight road to man. Had the law of variation worked only in one direction, man might have found himself the sole occupant of the universe. Behold the varieties of trees, of shrubs, of grasses, of birds, of insects, because Nature does not work as man does, with an eye single to one particular end. She scatters, she sows her seed upon the wind, she commits her germs to the waves and the floods. Nature is indifferent to waste, because what goes out of one pocket goes into another. She is indifferent to failure, because failure on one line means success on some other.

IV

But I am not preaching much of a gospel, am I? Only the gospel of contentment, of appreciation, of heeding simple near-by things—a gospel the burden of which still is love, but love that goes hand in hand with understanding.

There is so much in Nature that is lovely and lovable, and so much that gives us pause. But here it is, and here we are, and we must make the most of it. If the ways of the Eternal as revealed in his works are past finding out, we must still unflinchingly face what our reason reveals to us. "Red in tooth and claw." Nature does not preach; she enforces, she executes. All her answers are yea, yea, or nay, nay. Of the virtues and beatitudes of which the gospel of Christ makes so much—meekness, forgiveness, self-denial, charity, love, holiness—she knows nothing. Put yourself in her way, and she crushes you; she burns you, freezes you, stings you, bites you, or devours you.

Yet I would not say that the study of Nature did not favor meekness or sobriety or gentleness or forgiveness or charity, because the great Nature students and prophets, like Darwin, would rise up and confound me. Certainly it favors seriousness, truthfulness, and simplicity of life; or, are only the serious and single-minded drawn to the study of Nature? I doubt very much if it favors devoutness or holiness, as those qualities are inculcated by the church, or any form of religious enthusiasm. Devoutness and holiness come of an attitude toward the universe that is in many ways incompatible with that implied by the pursuit of natural science. The joy of the Nature student like Darwin or any great naturalist is to know, to find out the reason of things and the meaning of things, to trace the footsteps of the creative energy; while the religious devotee is intent only upon losing himself in infinite being. True, there have been devout naturalists and men of science; but their devoutness did not date from their Nature studies, but from their training, or from the times in which they lived. Theology and science, it must be said, will not mingle much better than oil and water, and your devout scientist and devout Nature student lives in two separate compartments of his being at different times. Intercourse with Nature—I mean intellectual intercourse, not merely the emotional intercourse of the sailor or explorer or farmer—tends to beget a habit of mind the farthest possible removed from the myth-making, the vision-seeing, the voice-hearing habit and temper. In all matters relating to the visible, concrete universe it substitutes broad daylight for twilight; it supplants fear with curiosity; it overthrows superstition with fact; it blights credulity with the frost of skepticism. I say frost of skepticism advisedly. Skepticism is a much more healthful and robust habit of mind than the limp, pale-blooded, non-resisting habit that we call credulity.

In intercourse with Nature you are dealing with things at first hand, and you get a rule, a standard, that serves you through life. You are dealing with primal sanities, primal honesties, primal attraction; you are touching at least the hem of the garment with which the infinite is clothed, and virtue goes out from it to you. It must be added that you are dealing with primal cruelty, primal blindness, primal wastefulness, also. Nature works with reference to no measure of time, no bounds of space, and no limits of material. Her economies are not our economies. She is prodigal, she is careless, she is indifferent; yet nothing is lost. What she lavishes with one hand, she gathers in with the other. She is blind, yet she hits the mark because she shoots in all directions. Her germs fill the air; the winds and the tides are her couriers. When you think you have defeated her, your triumph is hers; it is still by her laws that you reach your end.

We make ready our garden in a season, and plant our seeds and hoe our crops by some sort of system. Can any one tell how many hundreds of millions of years Nature has been making ready her garden and planting her seeds?

There can be little doubt, I think, but that intercourse with Nature and a knowledge of her ways tends to simplicity of life. We come more and more to see through the follies and vanities of the world and to appreciate the real values. We load ourselves up with so many false burdens, our complex civilization breeds in us so many false or artificial wants, that we become separated from the real sources of our strength and health as by a gulf.

For my part, as I grow older I am more and more inclined to reduce my baggage, to lop off superfluities. I become more and more in love with simple things and simple folk—a small house, a hut in the woods, a tent on the shore. The show and splendor of great houses, elaborate furnishings, stately halls, oppress me, impose upon me. They fix the attention upon false values, they set up a false standard of beauty; they stand between me and the real feeders of character and thought. A man needs a good roof over his head winter and summer, and a good chimney and a big wood-pile in winter. The more open his four walls are, the more fresh air he will get, and the longer he will live.

How the contemplation of Nature as a whole does take the conceit out of us! How we dwindle to mere specks and our little lives to the span of a moment in the presence of the cosmic bodies and the interstellar spaces! How we hurry! How we husband our time! A year, a month, a day, an hour may mean so much to us. Behold the infinite leisure of Nature!

A few trillions or quadrillions of years, what matters it to the Eternal? Jupiter and Saturn must be billions of years older than the earth. They are evidently yet passing through that condition of cloud and vapor and heat that the earth passed through untold aeons ago, and they will not reach the stage of life till aeons to come. But what matters it? Only man hurries. Only the Eternal has infinite time. When life comes to Jupiter, the earth will doubtless long have been a dead world. It may continue a dead world for aeons longer before it is melted up in the eternal crucible and recast, and set on its career of life again.

Familiarity with the ways of the Eternal as they are revealed in the physical universe certainly tends to keep a man sane and sober and safeguards him against the vagaries and half-truths which our creeds and indoor artificial lives tend to breed. Shut away from Nature, or only studying her through religious fears and superstitions, what a mess a large body of mankind in all ages have made of it! Think of the obsession of the speedy "end of the world" which has so often taken possession of whole communities, as if a world that has been an eternity in forming could end in a day, or on the striking of the clock! It is not many years since a college professor published a book figuring out, from some old historical documents and predictions, just the year in which the great mundane show would break up. When I was a small boy at school in the early forties, during the Millerite excitement about the approaching end of all mundane things, I remember, on the day when the momentous event was expected to take place, how the larger school-girls were thrown into a great state of alarm and agitation by a thundercloud that let down a curtain of rain, blotting out the mountain on the opposite side of the valley. "There it comes!" they said, and their tears flowed copiously. I remember that I did not share their fears, but watched the cloud, curious as to what the end of the world would be like. I cannot brag, as Thoreau did, when he said he would not go around the corner to see the world blow up. I am quite sure my curiosity would get the better of me and that I should go, even at this late day. Or think of the more harmless obsession of many good people about the second coming of Christ, or about the resurrection of the physical body when the last trumpet shall sound. A little natural knowledge ought to be fatal to all such notions. Natural knowledge shows us how transient and insignificant we are, and how vast and everlasting the world is, which was aeons before we were, and will be other aeons after we are gone, yea, after the whole race of man is gone. Natural knowledge takes the conceit out of us, and is the sure antidote to all our petty anthropomorphic views of the universe.

V

I was struck by this passage in one of the recently published letters of Saint-Gaudens: "The principal thought in my life is that we are on a planet going no one knows where, probably to something higher (on the Darwinian principle of evolution); that, whatever it is, the passage is terribly sad and tragic, and to bear up at times against what seems to be the Great Power that is over us, the practice of love, charity, and courage are the great things."

The "Great Power" that is over us does seem unmindful of us as individuals, if it does not seem positively against us, as Saint-Gaudens seemed to think it was.

Surely the ways of the Eternal are not as our ways. Our standards of prudence, of economy, of usefulness, of waste, of delay, of failure—how far off they seem from the scale upon which the universe is managed or deports itself! If the earth should be blown to pieces to-day, and all life instantly blotted out, would it not be just like what we know of the cosmic prodigality and indifference? Such appalling disregard of all human motives and ends bewilders us.

Of all the planets of our system probably only two or three are in a condition to sustain life. Mercury, the youngest of them all, is doubtless a dead world, with absolute zero on one side and a furnace temperature on the other. But what matters it? Whose loss or gain is it? Life seems only an incident in the universe, evidently not an end. It appears or it does not appear, and who shall say yea or nay? The asteroids at one time no doubt formed a planet between Mars and Jupiter. Some force which no adjective can describe or qualify blew it into fragments, and there, in its stead, is this swarm of huge rocks making their useless rounds in the light of the sun forever and ever. What matters it to the prodigal All? Bodies larger than our sun collide in the depths of space before our eyes with results so terrific that words cannot even hint them. The last of these collisions—of this "wreck of matter and crush of worlds"—reported itself to our planet in February, 1901, when a star of the twelfth magnitude suddenly blazed out as a star of the first magnitude and then slowly faded. It was the grand finale of the independent existence of two enormous celestial bodies. They apparently ended in dust that whirled away in the vast abyss of siderial space, blown by the winds upon which suns and systems drift as autumn leaves. It would be quite in keeping with the observed ways of the Eternal, if these bodies had had worlds in their train, teeming with life, which met the same fate as the central colliding bodies.

Does not force as we know it in this world go its own way with the same disregard of the precious thing we call life? Such long and patient preparations for it,—apparently the whole stellar system in labor pains to bring it forth,—and yet held so cheaply and indifferently in the end! The small insect that just now alighted in front of my jack-plane as I was dressing a timber, and was reduced to a faint yellow stain upon the wood, is typical of the fate of man before the unregarding and unswerving terrestrial and celestial forces. The great wheels go round just the same whether they are crushing the man or crushing the corn for his bread. It is all one to the Eternal. Flood, fire, wind, gravity, are for us or against us indifferently. And yet the earth is here, garlanded with the seasons and riding in the celestial currents like a ship in calm summer seas, and man is here with all things under his feet. All is well in our corner of the universe. The great mill has made meal of our grist and not of the miller. We have taken our chances and have won. More has been for us than against us. During the little segment of time that man has been upon the earth, only one great calamity that might be called cosmical has befallen it. The ice age of one or two hundred thousand years was such a calamity. But man survived it. The spring came again, and life, the traveler, picked itself up and made a new start. But if he had not survived it, if nothing had survived it, the great procession would have gone on just the same; the gods would have been just as well pleased.

The battle is to the strong, the race is to the fleet. This is the order of nature. No matter for the rest, for the weak, the slow, the unlucky, so that the fight is won, so that the race of man continues. You and I may fail and fall before our time; the end may be a tragedy or a comedy. What matters it? Only some one must succeed, will succeed.

We are here, I say, because, in the conflict of forces, the influences that made for life have been in the ascendant. This conflict of forces has been a part of the process of our development. We have been ground out as between an upper and a nether millstone, but we have squeezed through, we have actually arrived, and are all the better for the grinding—all those who have survived. But, alas for those whose lives went out in the crush! Maybe they often broke the force of the blow for us.

Nature is not benevolent; Nature is just, gives pound for pound, measure for measure, makes no exceptions, never tempers her decrees with mercy, or winks at any infringement of her laws. And in the end is not this best? Could the universe be run as a charity or a benevolent institution, or as a poor-house of the most approved pattern? Without this merciless justice, this irrefragable law, where should we have brought up long ago? It is a hard gospel; but rocks are hard too, yet they form the foundations of the hills.

Man introduces benevolence, mercy, altruism, into the world, and he pays the price in his added burdens; and he reaps his reward in the vast social and civic organizations that were impossible without these things.

I have no doubt that the life of man upon this planet will end, as all other forms of life will end. But the potential man will continue and does continue on other spheres. One cannot think of one part of the universe as producing man, and no other part as capable of it. The universe is all of a piece so far as its material constituents are concerned; that we know. Can there be any doubt that it is all of a piece so far as its invisible and intangible forces and capabilities are concerned? Can we believe that the earth is an alien and a stranger in the universe? that it has no near kin? that there is no tie of blood, so to speak, between it and the other planets and systems? Are the planets not all of one family, sitting around the same central source of warmth and life? And is not our system a member of a still larger family or tribe, and it of a still larger, all bound together by ties of consanguinity? Size is nothing, space is nothing. The worlds are only red corpuscles in the arteries of the infinite. If man has not yet appeared on the other planets, he will in time appear, and when he has disappeared from this globe, he will still continue elsewhere.

I do not say that he is the end and aim of creation; it would be logical, I think, to expect a still higher form. Man has been man but a little while comparatively, less than one hour of the twenty-four of the vast geologic day; a few hours more and he will be gone; less than another geologic day like the past, and no doubt all life from the earth will be gone. What then? The game will be played over and over again in other worlds, without approaching any nearer the final end than we are now. There is no final end, as there was no absolute beginning, and can be none with the infinite.

THE END

Printed in Great Britain
by Amazon